More praise for Paula Fox's *The Widow's Children*

"Paula Fox is so good a novelist that one wants to go out in the street to hustle up a big audience for her. . . . Mortification, humiliation, unattended gasps for recognition—Fox spares her characters no distress. . . . Fox's brilliance has a masochistic aspect: I will do this so well, she seems to say, that you will hardly be able to read it. And so she does, and so do I."
—Peter S. Prescott, *Newsweek*

"Paula Fox's remarkable alertness to human weakness enables her to portray an unpleasant family with the convincing clarity of a brilliantly unflattering photograph. . . . Shattering."
—T. R. Edwards, *Harper's*

"With considerable skill, Fox moves her characters through the long, continuous scene that makes up the main body of the novel. From a room in a hotel, through its corridors, into streets and thence into a restaurant, this tightly stuck-together group performs a kind of dance of death from which now an arm protrudes, now a leg or a distorted face. Because of her skill, the reader reads and hopes."
—Norma Rosen, *New York Times Book Review*

"A splendid novel. . . . A work of marvelous design and subtle synchronization, returning the novel to its proper domain, real people, invested with a life they've been denied elsewhere."
—*Kirkus Reviews*

"Demonstrates once again Fox's original unsettling talent. . . . Astounding in its portrayal of the textures of emotional life, moment by agonizing moment. . . . Fox releases conflicts and passions of great intensity, and sets them simmering, combining, and exploding like volatile liquid elements."
—L. S. Schwartz, *Saturday Review*

"A drama of rival presences and outlooks. . . . A compelling and satisfying book. . . . It has in it, especially apparent in the wit, a worldliness which it could not do without, and which is that of someone who has lived long enough to have learned a good deal. . . . Remarkable." —Karl Miller, *New York Review of Books*

Books by Paula Fox

Novels
Poor George
Desperate Characters
The Western Coast
The Widow's Children
A Servant's Tale
The God of Nightmares

Books for children
How Many Miles to Babylon?
The Stone-Faced Boy
Portrait of Ivan
Blowfish Live in the Sea
The Slave Dancer
A Place Apart
One-eyed Cat
The Moonlight Man
Lily and the Lost Boy
The Village by the Sea
Monkey Island
Amzat and his Brothers
The Little Swineherd and Other Tales
Western Wind
The Eagle Kite
Radiance Descending

The Widow's Children

by
Paula Fox

Introduction by Andrea Barrett

W. W. NORTON & COMPANY
New York • London

For Brewster Board, Marjorie Kellogg, and
Gillian Jagger

Copyright © 1976, 1986 by Paula Fox
Introduction copyright © 1999 by Andrea Barrett

First published as a Norton paperback 1999

The lines from "Widow" quoted as the epigraph appear in Rainer Maria
Rilke's *Poems 1906–1926,* translated by J. B. Leishman, copyright © 1957
by New Directions Publishing Corporation. Reprinted by permission of New
Directions Publishing Corporation.

With thanks to the John Simon Guggenheim Memorial Foundation and the
National Endowment for the Arts for their support in the writing of this
book.

Library of Congress Cataloging in Publication Data

Fox, Paula.
   The widow's children / by Paula Fox ; introduction by Andrea Barrett.
      p. cm.
   ISBN 0-393-31963-6 pbk.
      1. Hispanic Americans—New York (State)—New York Fiction.
   I. Title.
   PS3556.094W5   1999
813'.54—dc21   99-38698
                                                        CIP

W. W. Norton & Company, Inc.
500 Fifth Avenue, New York, N.Y. 10110
www.wwnorton.com

W. W. Norton & Company Ltd.
10 Coptic Street, London WC1A 1PU

2 3 4 5 6 7 8 9 0

"Deprived of their first leaves her barren children stand, and seem, for all the world, to have been born because she pleased some terror . . . ."
"Widow"—Rainer Maria Rilke

The Old Beasts:
On *The Widow's Children*

Introduction by Andrea Barrett

Imagine the characters of a Greek tragedy—one that strictly obeys the Aristotelian unities of time and place—transposed to a short novel set in New York City in the early 1970s. Imagine they brilliantly illuminate that place and time, even while apparently focused on their persistent grievances, their needs for revenge, their contradictory yearnings for chaos and order, and their struggles for identity. Imagine, then, that their creator is gifted with absolute insight into each of them, male and female, old and young; that she possesses wit as well as the fiercest intelligence; that she has a deadly good ear and a prose style as sharp and precise as the bit of a drill.

Imagine all this, if you can—and still, you won't have grasped this astringent, moving novel. I don't pretend to understand it. But I am inspired by its rigorous intelligence, its elegant structure, its economy, and its passion.

The Widow's Children was first published in 1976. By then, Paula Fox, who was born in 1923, had already written nearly a dozen well-received novels for children (the best-known of these, *The Slave Dancer,* won the 1974 Newbery Medal) and three excellent novels for adults. We ought to be as familiar with these as we are with the similarly brilliant works of Fox's contemporaries Iris Murdoch, Muriel Spark, and Flannery O'Connor. Yet somehow they have not yet entered the canon in the same way.

Desperate Characters, Fox's best novel before *The Widow's Children,* was published in 1970; after a film based on it was made, a paperback edition enjoyed a brief popular life but soon went out of print. Reissued in 1980, it later went out of print again: it's finally available now, after more than a decade. How did we lose track of it? Irving Howe, in his afterword to the 1980 reissue, placed *Desperate Characters* squarely within "a major American tradition, the line of the short novel exemplified by *Billy Budd, The Great Gatsby, Miss Lonelyhearts,* and *Seize the Day*": a tradition in which "everything—action, form, language—is fiercely compressed, and often enough, dark-grained as well."

Useful words, which apply not only to *Desperate Characters* but also to *The Widow's Children.* A little over two hundred pages long, it is beautifully, ruthlessly compact, dependent on an absolute precision about character, emotion, and those violent familial bonds that Willa Cather, writing in praise of Katherine Mansfield, once described as

> secret and passionate and intense—which is the real life that
> stamps the faces and gives character to the voices of our
> friends. Always in his mind each member of these social units
> is escaping, running away, trying to break the net which cir-
> cumstances and his own affections have woven about him.
> One realizes that human relationships are the tragic neces-
> sity of human life; that they can never be wholly satisfacto-
> ry, that every ego is half the time greedily seeking them, and
> half the time pulling away from them.

I don't invoke those names casually—Fox shares Cather's elegant lucidity and Mansfield's uncanny insight into the subterranean stream of human relationships, while having her own ferocious bite.

Despite its abundant riches, and Fox's long and successful track record, *The Widow's Children* evoked bewilderment as well as praise when it was first published. A few reviewers were grouchy—one called it "a strange, bilious novel about a violent family gathering"—while others, admiring, were still baffled by "the extraordinary difficulty one encounters in trying to describe it. . . . [A]djectives, plot summaries, and character analyses leave out almost everything that is singular about *The Widow's Children.*" The fates have been unkind to it; reissued once before, in 1986, it has been out of print since 1990 and remains obdurately resistant to dissection.

This strikes me as one sure sign of its enduring brilliance— like a poem, it cannot be anatomized in any terms other than its own. Every line, every word, is there for a reason—yet it lives and breathes, it has not succumbed to the airlessness of perfection. Powerful, upsetting, it is also peculiarly exhilarating in its formal beauties and in its insights—and is never, ever depressing. In an interview, Fox once remarked:

> People are always saying that my work is *"depressing."* But what does that mean? . . . I'm so used to having the word *"depressing"* tied to me I feel like a dog accustomed to the tin can around its neck. The charge can still make me angry, not because of how it might reflect on my work, but because of what it tells me about reading in this country. Is *Anna Karenina* depressing? Is *Madame Bovary*? "Depressing," when applied to a literary work, is so narrow, so confining, so impoverished and impoverishing. This yearning for the proverbial "happy ending" is little more than a desire for oblivion.

You will find no oblivion here. Nor will you find what the narrator of Fox's fine 1990 novel, *The God of Nightmares,* scorns as "importunate and bullying optimism, and the hardened heart which was its consequence." Instead you'll find the most bracing clarity.

The Widow's Children is built, unusually, from seven chapters of unequal length, laconically titled "Drinks," "Corridor," "Restaurant," "The Messenger," "The Brothers," "Clara," and "The Funeral." Five characters form the cast: Laura Maldonada Clapper, a fifty-five-year-old faded beauty, twice-married, daughter of the impoverished widow, Alma; Laura's feckless, hard-drinking husband, Desmond; her timid, self-loathing daughter Clara; her brother Carlos, openly gay and a failed music critic; and her old friend, a squelched book editor named Peter Rice.

The arc of their actions is simple, almost trivial. Alma, shuffled off to a nursing home and neglected, has died on the day before Laura and Desmond are scheduled to leave for a trip to Africa. Laura is notified of the death by phone, but conceals the information from everyone. That evening, Clara, Carlos, and Peter join Laura and Desmond for an uneasy *bon voyage*: the novel opens in the hotel room where they meet, and explores with Proustian intensity, over the course of some eighty pages, the characters' interactions within that confined space. Later they inch down a corridor, move through the bleak rainy streets, and settle into a garish restaurant, where their conversation reflects only the most distorted surface of their underlying passions and secrets. Without warning, everything comes to a head in a huge messy outburst of Laura's.

After the characters separate, "The Messenger" (an important character in many Greek plays), enters. In this case he's played by Peter, who's been charged to carry the news of Alma's death to Carlos (whom Laura avoided telling all evening) and to their brother Eugenio (who has been absent). Peter has also been commanded not to tell Clara this vital news. In a swirl of accusations and recriminations, thought-less actions and sleep-deprived conversations, the final move-ment unrolls swiftly through a long dark night of the soul and into Alma's funeral the following day.

That's it, on the surface. But this is like saying that *What Maisie Knew*—to the spirit of which this novel bears some kinship—is about a child caught in a messy divorce. What's important is what's going on *underneath:* what the characters don't say, to each other or to themselves; what they are think-ing, what they feel; the long secret history of their uprooted, once-Spanish, family. The intensity of those subterranean movements is part of what has kept the novel from dating. Even now it feels startlingly contemporary in its acceptance of multiple forms of sexuality, its sharp focus on the nature of identity and the costs of exile, and its grasp of what we now label "dysfunctional families."

There is real, and unexpected, suspense in Fox's subtle working-out of the shifting configurations of these family rela-tionships. Equally compelling is the pattern of rootlessness established by Alma's displacement from Spain to Cuba, and then to New York, which resonates through three genera-tions. As the characters struggle with the paralysis induced by resentment and old grudges, the memory of poverty and the pain of exile, they, and we, are caught in a storm that's light-ened at the most surprising moments by shafts of humor and by the characters' fierce, amazing bursts of self-awareness.

This is especially true in the novel's long first chapter, which allows us to experience the hour in that hotel room much as the characters do. We share with them, because we're meant to, a sense of feeling trapped, itchy, uneasy; we *feel* the slowness with which time passes during their endless arguments. We experience—as we might in our own lives, although at a more muted level—what Clara thinks of as the

horrible "discrepancy between surface talk and inner preoccupation." Yet even as we're privy to the grinding, repetitive
nature of these characters' arguments (this is the part that's
like life), we also plunge into the limpid, lonely purity of their
thoughts. (This is what makes it art.) One by one, we come to
know them.

First, Laura. Receiving the news that her mother has died,
she immediately conceals this from her husband, and thinks
about hiding it from everyone else as well:

> Her mind had been empty of thought; she had known only
> that something implacable had taken hold of her. And she
> had felt a half-crazed pleasure and an impulse to shout that
> she knew and possessed this thing that no one else knew, this
> consequential fact, hard and real among the soft accumula-
> tions of meaningless events of which their planned trip to
> Africa was one other, to be experienced only through its
> arrangements, itinerary, packing, acquisition of medicines
> for intestinal upsets, books to read, clock, soap, passports,
> this husk of action surrounding the motionless center of their
> existence together.

Then Carlos, with his urbane matters and seemingly imper-
turbable surface, unaware that his mother is already dead:

> Waking at a late hour of a Sunday morning, knowing he ought
> to visit his mother at the home, knowing that he would not,
> aware of the noxious stink of his apartment, of stale food and
> dust and unwashed sheets, Carlos would fold his hands
> behind his head and lie there, tears running down his cheeks,
> thinking of his used-up life, of lovers dead or gone, of invest-
> ments made unwisely, of his violent sister who might tele-
> phone him at any minute and, with her elaborate killer's
> manners, in her beautiful deep voice, make some outrageous
> demand upon him, making clear she knew not only the open
> secrets of his life but the hidden ones, knew about his real
> shiftlessness, his increasing boredom with sexual pursuit, his

unappeased sexual longing, his terror of age. "I'm becoming an old sow," he would whisper to himself, trying to keep at bay the thought of his mother waiting in the disinfectant, linoleum-smelling stillness of the old people's home for him to come and see her.

Drifting between them is Desmond, already deeply drunk; thinking inappropriately and yet believably about a salesgirl with "a flat rear end, buttocks hanging down like frying pans." And buttressing that trio, linked by fear and timidity, are Clara (abandoned by Laura at birth, and raised by Alma) and Peter, ironic and reserved.

Of Peter we have, in this brilliantly orchestrated first chapter, thoughts less revealing of his inner state—perhaps because, in one of the novel's great surprises, the last three chapters are turned over almost entirely to him. In the fourth, central chapter—very short, and functioning as a hinge between the two other groups of three—the news of Alma's death is passed from Laura to Desmond to Peter, who is asked to bring that message to the remainder of the family. Only with this switch in perspective do we see the Maldonadas fully, from the outside: their effects on others, all they have caused, all their sufferings. Only here do we learn the full, heartbreaking history of Alma, the secrets of Carlos and Eugenio, and the devastating effects of this family on Peter. Although we couldn't have suspected it at first, Peter is far from a minor character. Not the book's hero—the book has no heroes—but a consciousness central to our vision.

Until that crucial fourth chapter, everyone has been reacting to Laura, fearing Laura, hiding from her, attempting to please her. Her mind is closed to us after the opening pages; we know her only through what she says and how the others respond to her until, in the final movement of "Restaurant," she reacts with an outburst of emotion to an innocent comment of Clara's. Leaping from the table, hurling herself into the streets, she is frantic. In those moments we get our sole crucial glimpse of the interior life of the woman who has, for Peter, represented all that is chaotic and free and wild, all the life he has denied himself:

> That girl! That girl with her open mouth, her idiot fearfulness—and Peter Rice, an insect husk, the goddamned vampire sucking her life away, that bloodless Christian sewing machine with his intolerable daintiness—what *had she* to do with such creatures, what did she have to do with thick-witted, thick-ankled old Desmond and his infant thieving of liquor, or with debauched Carlos—but at the thought of Carlos, Laura began to cry. She didn't understand *anything*! The unyielding mystery of her impulses was punishment enough for whatever she had done—she thought she had put them to sleep so long ago, that they had withered away just as she was withering away, but they were awake, the old beasts of her life, so merciless, so cruel. . . . An enormous grief rose in her. The knowledge of the death of her mother flooded her bloodstream, entered her bowels, her marrow.

It is this woman—a woman who thinks of him as a "bloodless Christian sewing machine"—to whom Peter has devoted his life. For thirty years he has held, against all competing evidence, his first vision of her:

> He had not known Carlos well, then, and he had never known a Spaniard before. Here were Spaniards. Laura in the light, clear air like a dark root, slender then, balancing her peony head, sitting quietly in a chintz-covered chair, the sunlight falling upon the rug at her feet and on the legs of the white rattan table on the edge of which her cigarette burned.

There's nothing I can add to a passage like that; truly, this novel can't be described. All I can do is offer tidbits, and suggest that its narrative voice and structure, so unusual at first glance, exist in part to make possible the bloody glimpses inside the characters. It's as if they've been trepanned, or have trepanned themselves. It's as if, through the holes bored into this contentious group, Fox has illuminated the stony path stretching between their (our) adult selves and the snow-strewn childhood morning Peter remembers, when he woke and "felt that that day, he only wanted to be good."

I haven't talked about the subtle, brilliant way that Alma's history and Clara's childhood are revealed in fragments, through the conversations and memories of the other characters. Neither have I done justice to the mysterious Eugenio, as complicated and touching as all the others, though he enters so late. I should talk about Fox's gorgeous prose, her ability to orchestrate tempo, and her mastery (she has, among contemporary writers, no equals in this) of point-of-view. I've scanted the extraordinary *rightness* of Fox's imagery, which recurs and rebounds in troubling patterns, as in a dream or a nightmare: the way, for example, that the violent Maldonadas view people in terms of animals—cats, tigers, opossums, porcupines—while Peter, and only Peter, sees them in terms of flowers and vegetables: Laura, above all, with her "peony head."

There is, too, the skill with which Fox reveals the corrosive sadness of late middle age, the deceptions and self-deceptions of love, the long secret paths by which, as Laura notes, we change: "We all do, we grow disfigured and hideous like my poor mother's black shoes." And there is so much else, so much else—but to talk about it all is to quote, in the end, every line in the book. I've pulled out of context fragments I find singularly piercing, but all that surrounds those lines is equally piercing. The novel is itself, wholly itself; there is no way to comprehend it except to read it.

—June 1999

The Widow's Children

CHAPTER ONE

Drinks

Clara Hansen, poised upright in her underwear on the edge of a chair, was motionless. Soon she must turn on a light. Soon she must finish dressing. She would permit herself three more minutes in her darkening apartment in that state that was so nearly sleep. She turned to face a table on which sat a small alarm clock. At once, a painful agitation brought her to her feet. She would be late; buses were not reliable. She could not afford a taxi to take her to the hotel where her mother, Laura, and Laura's husband, Desmond Clapper, were expecting her for drinks and dinner. In the morning, the Clappers were sailing away on a ship—this time, to Africa. They would be gone for months. Clara had managed to get away from the office where she worked a half hour early so she would have time enough. But it had been time enough to fall into a dream of nothingness.

Clara went quickly to her small bedroom where her dress lay across the bed. It was the best thing she owned. She was aware that as a rule she dressed defensively. But she had made a perverse choice for this evening. Laura would know the dress was expensive. The hell with it, she told herself, but felt only irresoluteness as the silk settled against her skin.

A few drops of rain slid down the windows as she passed through the living room. She turned on a light to come home to, and for a brief moment, it seemed the evening was already over, that she had returned, consoled by the knowledge that once Laura was gone, she hardly need think of her. After all, the occasions of their meetings were so rare.

It was early April and still cold, but Clara put on a light raincoat. It was shabby and soiled, but it suited some in-tention—a repudiation of the dress—of which Clara was only remotely aware.

Clara's uncle, Carlos, would be there. And Laura had said on the phone that an editor friend was coming along for this farewell evening. Clara had met him once long ago; she did not think anything about him. As she walked along the street, she saw a bus coming and she hastened toward the stop. She felt at once, as though her hurrying feet had brought it on, a distressed excitement, the mood in which she always entered her mother's territory.

A dozen blocks south from Clara's apartment house, in an old brownstone off Lexington Avenue, Carlos Mal-donada, Laura's brother, stood next to his sink holding a wizened lemon in his hand. He didn't especially want the vodka he had poured out for himself. He dropped the lemon which fell into the sink and lodged among the dirty dishes, then wandered off to his closet. Without bothering to look, he took a jacket from out of the musty dark and put it on.

He started toward the telephone. He could tell Laura he

had tripped on a curb and hurt his ankle. It would have to
be a detailed story—what he had slipped on, the passerby
who had helped him, the degree of swelling, how he'd
managed to get back to his apartment, the hours soaking
the ankle in a basin—he didn't have a basin—the pain-
killers he'd taken.

"You damned wicked old liar!" he said, imitating Laura's
voice exactly, and laughed to hear his words in the dusty,
cluttered room. He found his beret and a coat, swallowed
the vodka on his way past the kitchen counter, and hurried down the stairs to the sidewalk where a taxi drew up
just as he raised his arm. But once he was slumped on the
cracked vinyl seat, his feet among wet cigarette butts, Carlos's energy faltered. He gave the address of the Clappers'
hotel in a dispirited voice and did not respond to the cabdriver's remarks, even though he was a young cabdriver
and very good-looking.

The Clappers' third guest, Peter Rice, was still in his office. With a red pencil, he checked his name in a list of editors on a memo attached to an English magazine. He had
not looked at it; he didn't read magazines of any kind
anymore. His secretary, her coat draped around her shoulders, brought him the package of books he had requested.
He signed a slip, smiled, thanked her, wished her a pleasant weekend, saw from his window a tugboat on the East
River far below, and regretted, as he noticed the rain
beginning to fall, that he had not brought his umbrella
with him in the morning. It was only a formal regret; he
didn't pay attention to weather in the city.

He hadn't seen Laura for a year. They spoke on the
phone from time to time. It was Laura who called him

from the Clapper farm in Pennsylvania. No one else telephoned him late in the evening, so when the phone rang,
he always picked it up with a start of pleasure, knowing it
would be she. This last year all her conversations had
begun in despair and drama—lurid tales of Desmond's
drinking. But after a while she would grow calm, and they
would speak together as they always had.

He reached for his hat. In the corridor a woman
laughed. He heard footsteps going toward the elevators.
The tugboat had disappeared from view. He turned off his
desk lamp. The watery half-light of dusk flooded into his
office but did not dim the shining jackets of the books
lined up on the shelves. A worrying sense that a day had
passed without leaving a mark kept him standing there,
feeling lifeless. Then he thought of Laura. He picked up
the package of books and left.

In the hotel bathroom, Desmond Clapper was staring at
his reddening fingers as the tap water poured over them.
The rush of water did not quite drown out Laura's voice.
In a moment, he would have to go into the bedroom to her.
He turned the taps off, then on again.

"Tell me about the dignity of leopards! Of cockroaches!
But don't tell me about the dignity of man! How dare anybody stop anybody from going anyplace in the goddamned
world? I was nearly in the restaurant when I saw you on
the other side of that picket line, looking foolish, while
those waiters scuttled back and forth between us mum-
bling about their grievances. . . ."

Desmond ground his teeth. She was still sore about
lunch. He couldn't help what had happened. The strikers
had cursed him every time he took a step toward Laura.

He listened. Then she started up again. But her voice seemed nearer. Could she be standing on the other side of the door?

"Desmond? Desmond! How *could* you have cared about crossing that picket line? Don't you know what waiters earn in a place like that? And—my God! Who has dignity in this life? It's only money they want . . . treat me like a man . . . throw me another dime! Do you remember those beggars in Madrid wheeled to the churches in carts by their children? And they shook their stumps at us and laughed? That was dignity! Desmond? We'd been looking forward so long to that lunch, and you grabbed me and forced me away. One of them had a sign that spelled *support* with one *p*. Did you notice that? Christ! I would have brought out a plate and eaten in front of them! The insolence! The stupidity! And the bookshop, that awful female clerk with her dirty fingernails, the wire of her brassiere sticking out through her shirt . . . and she *corrected* me. You must have known, all these years, that I mispronounced cupola. Why didn't you ever tell me? You know what a horror I have of mispronouncing English words. And she didn't exert herself to help us, pretending they had no new English detective stories in stock. You ought to call the manager of that place . . . letting people like that bully customers . . . letting them take out their frustrations on others. I asked her if she needed to use a toilet. Did you hear me ask her? I spoke quietly, which maddens such people. To think I've been saying *cupulow* all these years and no one said a word until that woman. I'm so jumpy! I think this drink will help. Desmond. I know I'm on a little rampage. Did you hear that? I know it. I'm not excusing myself. That's not the Spanish way. It's you

16

The Widow's Children

Anglos who specialize in piety. I never justify myself. Do I, Desmond? I'm not a Jew, after all. How I loathe self-pity! That brother of mine, that Carlos, has such a sentimental regard for his troubles—and oh, how he abandons us all, even my poor mother who prefers him to me and Eugenio. Desmond? If we could only leave without a word to a soul. When I called Clara, she told me she'd had a cold, with such a dying fall in her voice, and then showed how *brave* she was, saying, of course she wanted to see us before we sailed. If we could only just leave! Now! Cross the gangplank in the dark, slip into our cabin. The steward would bring us tea and biscuits, the ship would sail at midnight, no bands, no waving. God! Those *awful* waiters . . . I suppose they have dank lives, going home in the early morning hours on subways, too exhausted to add up their tips, carrying trays into their dreams . . . and that wretched clerk, no one bothering to tell her about her brassiere, no one to care about her breasts, after all. Look at the time! They'll all be here soon. I won't mind Peter. He understands an occasion, poor bastard. He and I, we've had over thirty years of occasions. My oldest friend . . . my only friend. Thank heaven I couldn't reach Eugenio. I can just imagine where he is, in the lair of some old woman secretly counting the real pearls around her throat, inflaming himself with the knowledge of how our family has fallen . . . fallen. . . ."

Now the rain began all at once as though flung at the hotel windows and on the black avenue eight stories below. Laura, looking down, could see wipers whipping across the windshields of the cars that filled the street, and the color of the traffic lights which ran in the rain, and the gleaming surface of the macadam awash with the violence

of the downpour. She lit a cigarette, then swallowed some
of her drink to moisten her dry mouth. She shuddered so
that even her legs trembled with the force of the spasm.
Almost at once, she pretended to wonder if there had been
an earthquake, if New York City was tumbling down, the
hotel crumbling beneath her, pretending that her convul-
sion had been visited upon her by an outside force and was
not what it must be, evidence of a prodigious fact she had
concealed throughout her harangue, during which, she
knew, Desmond had been turning the faucets on and off
to drown out her voice.

This fact was the news she had received when the Clappers had returned to the hotel from their final shopping for
the trip. The news was that her mother, Alma, had died in
midafternoon in a home for the elderly where she had
been living for the past two years. Laura had turned to
Desmond, even smiling when he asked her who was on
the telephone, replying it was Clara asking directions to
the hotel, would he unwrap the liquor bottles now? Then,
returning to the official gravity of the voice at the other
end of the wire, certification of death, it was saying, given
by the chief doctor on the staff—heart failed . . . quiet
death—asking about burial arrangements, and Laura had
called to Desmond, "Get me some aspirin, darling," and
had said hurriedly into the phone, "Tomorrow? Can it be
tomorrow? Whatever funeral people you use . . . yes . . .
but we have a plot, my husband arranged that with you
two years ago . . . on Long Island," and Desmond had
come back and handed her two aspirin, and she had said
into the phone, "Goodbye, I'll call you in the morning,"
and Desmond had said, "Call Clara? But she's coming
here tonight, isn't she?"

She hadn't been able to answer but he didn't press her; she could always count on Desmond's short interest span. Her mind had been empty of thought; she had known only that something implacable had taken hold of her. And she had felt a half-crazed pleasure and an impulse to shout that she knew and possessed this thing that no one else knew, this consequential fact, hard and real among the soft accumulations of meaningless events of which their planned trip to Africa was one other, to be experienced only through its arrangements, itinerary, packing, acquisition of medicines for intestinal upsets, books to read, clock, soap, passports, this husk of action surrounding the motionless center of their existence together.

Was Desmond drinking by himself in the bathroom? Getting in a few surreptitious swallows before the matron caught up with him? In a surge of fury at his cheating, his cowardice in appointing *her* the matron, she dropped her glass on the radiator against which it broke into several large pieces and fell to the carpet. Desmond appeared at once in the bathroom door, drying his hands with exaggerated care. She smiled, feeling a faint sweat on her upper lip. "Did you give the waiter a tip when he brought the ice? Oh, I dropped my glass."

"Darling, yes," he said. "Dropped your glass? I'll clean it up." He noticed a large smudge on her forehead and brushed at it with the edge of the towel, glancing past her at the window where, he guessed, she'd been leaning. "It's raining," he said. She laughed. "You couldn't have heard the rain over all that racket you were making in there," she said.

He smiled back, relieved at the composure of her voice. And he *had* listened to the part about going to the ship to-

night. He would certainly have liked *that* instead of the
wearisome and dangerous evening ahead. There was already broken glass—even if it was the result of an accident. Leopards, waiters, Jews, she wouldn't have gone
on so if her damned relatives weren't coming. He watched
her fold the towel she'd taken from him and then look into
the mirror on the wall above the chest of drawers. She'd
had her hair done that morning; it was piled on top of her
head. It was so gray! It continued to surprise him, that
middle-aged woman's hair. "What disgusting ringlets," she
said, her mirror eyes staring into his. He didn't care for
that stare, and he thought, I'll have a drink now. But as he
started toward the table where the bottles and glasses
were, he heard a tentative knock on the door, and he went
to it and opened it.

"I'm the first?" asked Clara Hansen, looking straight
past Desmond at her mother. His wasted smile lingered
around his lips.

"Hello," said Laura, bringing up the greeting from the
deepest reach of her voice, a plangent, thrilling annuncia-
tion to which, Clara knew, no response would measure up,
felt with a sinking heart that her own "hello" would weigh
less than dust on such a scale of tonal drama, and so only
held out her hand. Her mother gripped her fingers
strongly for an instant, then withdrew her hand to a cigarette.

"Doesn't she look marvelous!" exclaimed Laura. "Don't
men attack you on the street?"

"Clara, what will you have?" Desmond asked.

"Oh, Scotch," she said. "If you have it, and soda," and
kept her gaze on Desmond. Once they began to talk, she
and Laura, it would be all right. It would do. These first

moments were always harrowing, and she could not explain to herself the fright she felt, the conviction of peril.

She had not lived with Laura, or her father, Ed Hansen, not been under the same roof with her mother since that first parting twenty-nine years ago in a hospital delivery room. It was that, she told herself, it is because we never began and so must always start in the middle, a void forming just behind us. But this account of her relations with her mother, so exhilarating for a day, or an hour, did not hold. Between her and Laura there was no void but a presence, raw and bloodied. Laura had had four abortions before a fifth pregnancy which had gone undetected a month too long and had produced Clara. She had, she told herself, thieved her way into life.

"How are you, Miss?" Laura asked, perched now on the windowsill. "I wish you were coming with us. Don't you wish she was, Desmond? What a good time we'd have! Desmond, she wanted water, not soda."

"Did you say soda or water?" asked Desmond.

"Oh . . . either is fine," Clara said, "whatever comes to hand."

"But I thought you said water," Laura said intently.

"Actually, I think I said soda, but it doesn't matter. Really."

"Gosh, are you sure, Clara? Oh Christ! That must be Peter. I had hoped the three of us could have some time alone together, but—" and she went to open the door.

It was not Peter Rice but Carlos Maldonada.

"Carlos!"

"Hello, darling," said Carlos.

"Look who's here! Clara! Now, don't start up, you two," cried Laura gaily.

Carlos went directly to his niece and put his hand on her head and pressed his fingers upon her skull. She laughed immoderately.

"Any new jokes?" Carlos asked Clara.

"Oh, Carlos. My memory's getting so bad for jokes—"

"*Her* memory is getting bad!" exclaimed Laura, laughing. "At her age—"

"The goddamned waiter forgot the vermouth . . ." muttered Desmond.

"My dizzy Desmond," Laura murmured, "none of these gypsies would touch vermouth."

"I'll forgive you," said Carlos to Clara. "That last one! I'd forgive you anything for that!" *That* was an obscene joke she must have told him over a year ago, the last time she'd seen him, while they were walking up Lexington Avenue. He had laughed until he had cried. She hadn't thought the joke especially funny. But the laughter she'd brought up out of him—and not for the first time—had thrilled her; in the moment's blaze of his response, she'd been warmed. Yet what jokes took the place of, with their abject mangling of the ways of carnal life, their special language more stumps than words, she could not fathom. She tried now to remember something about a woman and a doorknob, something sufficiently coarse to evoke those cries and roars from them that would let her off the hook of their expectation for a few minutes. But her mother began to speak. Clara sighed with relief and swallowed too much liquor.

Laura was saying, "Gibraltar only for a day . . . then, Malaga for a week, then to Morocco, and we're actually ready to sail. We *were* ready—" and she paused suddenly and looked around the room as though utterly bewildered, as though searching for what she had been about to say written on a wall or a lampshade or a box on a table. The other three, pausing, too, in their consumption of liquor and smoke, heard the sound of the rain. It beat against the hotel windows. Clara held her breath. Then Desmond said, "I won't pay for that goddamned vermouth, of course. . . ." And Laura, who'd given them all the impression of someone twisting and turning in a dream, resumed speaking.

"We were ready. Then Desmond got a letter from his daughter, little Ellen, Ellie Bellie—you must see that letter, Clara! What a little sham she is! She wants to see her Daddy, she said, wants to talk about her career in publishing—which hasn't begun. Isn't she a little old to be beginning, darling? But Desmond, you must have told her that Peter Rice might help her get a job. You did, didn't you? You shouldn't encourage her hopes, you know. She writes like a twelve-year-old, and she must be thirty now. Isn't she? She's certainly older than Clara."

"Excuse me," said Desmond, and went into the bathroom.

"He is the champion wee-wee maker of seven continents," Laura remarked.

"I believe it's six continents," said Carlos.

"Thank God for your geographical lore, Carlos," Laura laughed. She was sitting on one of the twin beds. Carlos stood just behind her. The two Spaniards looked at Clara. Beneath their scrutiny the pain she had felt at the mention of that other girl, whom she'd never met, who, like herself, was no longer a girl, began to fade as though exposed to an obliterating light. She had the impression of two eagles swooping toward her. Oh—let them turn away! Yet, they were neither beaked nor birdlike, not with those massive northern Spanish heads. But she was pinioned by their gaze, its force doubled by their physical similarity, the same deep-set eyes beneath massive lid folds, the same large noses. Although Laura was gray-haired and Carlos nearly bald, they had about them something black, "Spanish," not quite human in the eyes above their smiling lips.

"You're not sailing?" Clara asked uncertainly, "because of Ellen . . . ?"

Laura laughed and shook her head as though in wonder at such a conclusion.

"Lovely legs," Carlos murmured with a charming smile, looking down at his niece's legs.

"And those hands," said Laura, "like a Renaissance page boy's. Oh! Look! She's blushing!" She rose from the bed and went over to Clara and chucked her under the chin. Clara smiled helplessly at Carlos and silently cursed her blood-reddened face. But it was not modesty that made her blush; it was anger at the injustice of a compliment that could only wound her.

During her adolescent years, she had been taken by her grandmother, Alma, to meet a ship, a train, to sit an hour or two in a hotel room or a restaurant with that fierce-looking foreign woman, her mother. In those days, she had tripped over her own feet, broken glasses of ginger ale and babbled hopelessly, waiting for Laura to say she had grown tall, had filled out, might someday even be pretty. Instead Laura told her her legs were exactly like Josephine Baker's, her round face like that of the boy in a Reynolds painting Laura had seen in London, that she had the look of a bacchante, and gathering up the fragments of glass she had broken—but the waiter always came so quickly, so grimly—hiding her gnawed fingernails beneath the napkin or the menu, trying, trying to shut her own damned mouth, she had gathered up, too, these descriptions of herself, this praise that left behind it a sense of insult and injury.

Now, she had Renaissance hands. She looked down at them covertly. One held a glass with a grip of stone. For an instant, and her heart leapt, she imagined herself standing, hurling the glass against the hotel windows. But the impulse vanished so quickly, she was hardly aware she had had it—only that her attention had wandered.

Laura was speaking of Ed Hansen, Clara's father, but with somewhat less contempt than she affected when Desmond was around. He was still in the bathroom. "But Clara told me—didn't you?—that Ed was awfully sick, not faking it this time, was it angina, Clara? And that Adelaide is trying to kick him out again. Is she tired of being the wonderful new wife? Or can't she stand his *art*? My God, Carlos! Did I tell you that time a few years ago when Ed called me—drunk as a lord—and said he was throwing out his cameras and going back to painting. Of course, he hasn't had to earn a living since he's been married to an heiress. Well . . . he was telling me about this painting thing, and suddenly on the phone, long distance, too, he began to cry, he said his heart was so full, you see, about being so old and finding painting all over again after all those lousy years of keeping us fed, keeping the rain off, he said, with the photography, and he was actually sobbing. But you know—old men, you can give them a cracker or tell them about a volcano erupting in a place they've never been and they'll cry just the way Ed was crying. He's not serious, that is the truth about him. He never was. That's why he was a good photographer."

"But he's not really an *old man*," Clara said.

"I suppose not," Laura replied, and looked at Carlos. "When did you see him last?" she asked.

"He—a few months ago, but he was drinking. I tried to make him eat something—"

Laura burst into laughter. "Oh, Carlos, *you* trying to make someone eat something—in that dunghill of a kitchen. . . . Darling! What did you give him? Coffee grounds and mouse droppings?"

"I just told you that the doctors said he was in very bad shape, and that if he didn't stop drinking, he wouldn't live long," Clara said loudly. "I don't know anything about Adelaide," she added.

"You don't, do you?" her mother said, staring at Clara, her eyes widening. "Well, how is he, apart from dying? When did you see him last, Clara?"

"Oh, it was months ago. But I spoke to him on the phone," Clara replied, then added hastily. "I phoned, to see how he was. And that last time I saw him, he wasn't sober. He didn't seem to know what he was doing . . . he gave me an old pocket watch of his, then the next morning, he called me and asked for it back."

"He was staying with me," Carlos said with a touch of defiance. "He was ashamed about the watch, Clarita."

"God! Isn't that typical!" said Laura. "And Clara, of course, gave it back. But tell me, how is Adelaide, the Queen of Pathos? You didn't know her well, Carlos. Or did you? My God! You never saw a woman so hell-bent on finding people to torment her. And when she does, how

she bears up! And then, a brave tear, a simple statement to
her admirers—'It's all my fault'—isn't that so, Clara? Clara
knows her, don't you, Missy?"

But Clara was spared the discomfort of replying by Desmond's emergence from the bathroom. Ed Hansen was
not to be mentioned in Desmond's presence. Laura had reported to her brother and daughter that he was subject to
terrible attacks of jealousy; he was demented, really, on
the subject of Ed, so much so, Laura claimed, that he
refused to speak to anyone named Edwin or Edmund or
Edward.

"Golly, I wonder where Peter is?" her mother said.

Clara went into the bathroom, thinking, gosh, golly, gee,
and why did Carlos and Laura use comic strip words? Who
were they condescending to? The United States? Who
were the Maldonadas? Immigrants, irate dependents per-
manently displaced by their own ceaseless effort to main-
tain a fiction of their distance from, their superiority over
the natives.

The bathroom was overheated. Among the rumpled tow-
els, lurking yet in the crumpled paper of a soap wrapper,
was the powerful smell of Desmond's urine. My God! A
drop of it might change the world! She visualized his black
mustache, beneath it, lips like old rubber bands. In there,
sheltered from Laura's scrutiny, she felt the strain of her
factitious animation drain away; she allowed herself to
long for the hours of this evening to pass, to disappear. On
these rare occasions when she saw Laura, or even her
uncles, Carlos and Eugenio, she suffered such confusion,
such a dislocation of self; wrenched out of her own life for
even a few hours, it seemed not to count, to be a dream
she could barely recall.

How had Desmond blundered into that coven? She
thought suddenly of her grandmother, Alma, who had
hatched the shocking brood. And Clara was stricken with
shame, for what excuses could she offer anyone to extenu-
ate her neglect of the old woman? But the shame was only
a pinch, a momentary sting. Already, inertia was separat-
ing her from resolution. Perhaps an impulse would rescue
her. Perhaps, one afternoon after work, she would find
herself approaching the home. For an instant, thinking of
Alma's pleasure when she arrived, Clara smiled. Almost at
once, the smile faded. Nothing, she realized, would make
her go, no mysterious, still unplumbed resource in her.

"I know many t'ings," her grandmother often avowed in
her heavily accented English. Her accent was phenome-
nal. For forty-five years, she had resisted learning English,
she, who had submitted to the brutal changes in her life
without contest, had defended the language she had been
born to, perhaps because it was the last connection with
that Iberian coast she had left at sixteen on a ship bound
for Cuba. She might know many things, but God knows
what they were! Her children never asked her what she
knew, but her phrase was repeated among them with
mocking amusement. Ed Hansen had asked her, and he'd
had no luck. "Ah Ed . . . many t'ings . . ." she'd sigh. Ed
had made her laugh, evoked in her a flirtatious gaiety.
Perhaps it had continued to astonish him that that dreamy,
forlorn woman had produced Laura and Carlos and
Eugenio.

Ed had charmed Alma from that first occasion Carlos
had brought him home on leave from the army training
depot where they'd been stationed during the First World
War. They had both been nineteen years old, and trying to

imagine what they'd been like—as she often did—Clara recalled a blurred snapshot she'd found in a shoebox in Alma's Brooklyn apartment. In it, Carlos stood languidly near a desk. Her father was smiling, his hand resting on Carlos's shoulder. How handsome they had been! How unimaginable that time would erode their grace! That Alma would, one day, wait for nothing in an old people's home.

She wet her hands in the sink, and dried them roughly. Of course, Laura knew she hadn't been to see Alma for five months. And if she didn't go for a year? What then? She felt a thrill of terror, but of what? What could Laura do?

She flushed the toilet several times. It would excuse her absence if anyone had noticed it. She had wanted a moment away from them, from the painful tension that Laura seemed to both produce and feed upon.

Clara opened the door. There was much cigarette smoke; the room felt smaller. Laura was lying on one of the twin beds, her head propped up on one hand, her hip curving up. Her body was not youthful but it wasn't matronly either. Laura was fifty-five.

She had just slipped her hand beneath the cover of a box which she was about to open. "Oh, Clara. I was just telling Carlos that Desmond bought me six dresses yesterday, all by himself. Can you imagine such a chap? Desmond . . . you're so good! But he's so bad! So extravagant!"

Carlos went to Clara and put his arm around her. "And I don't even have *one*," he whispered in her ear. She hugged him. He pressed his chin into her hair. They stretched out their hands. Laura said, "Look at those two, Desmond!"

Clara's and Carlos's hands were extraordinarily alike—it

was a joke between them. At least, it was something between them. They moved apart, Carlos laughing softly.
She felt uneasy. She cared about him, and these jokes,
these caresses, these eloquent but wordless signals, had
the effect of chilling her affection for him. He'd almost
always been kind to her. She loved his splendid walk—like
a tiger's, Ed had said, you would never have known he was
a pederast. Ed hadn't, he'd claimed, for years, and had let
her in on the secret when she'd been thirteen. She'd nodded calmly, concealing her ignorance of what he was talking about, knowing it was awful, terrified Carlos would
learn that she knew. That had been when she was con-
vinced the Maldonadas could read people's minds, espe
cially her own. But if Carlos had read her mind, it had not
affected his behavior toward her. In time, she had a revela-
tion. It was not his embarrassment she'd feared but her
own. Until a few years ago, Alma often said, "Ah, Carlos.
. . . Someday I hope he'll marry." She doted only on Carlos. About Eugenio she said nothing. And during all the
years of Clara's growing up, while Laura and Ed had
moved from Provence to Devon to Ibiza to Mexico, Alma
had rarely spoken of that spectral couple to whose existence foreign stamps gave witness (by the time one letter
arrived, they had often moved on to another place; Laura
never wrote, sending messages through Ed), saying only,
"Laurita es una viajera, eh?" with a kind of relentless
leniency, or saying something else as insubstantial, so that
the child, Clara, kept her questions to herself where, in the
fecund, lonely dark of adolescence, they grew monstrous.

But once in the world, she learned everyone's lesson—
families were not as they seemed; she grew artful in spot-
ting the cracks in domestic facades. Wasn't everyone dam-

aged? she asked herself, and read the ancient Greeks during the one year she'd gone to college, and concluded that the house of Atreus was, and always had been, full of boarders like herself. Then, a year ago, she had awakened one morning in a sweat of fear. Her life was a walk next to an electrified fence. The path was narrowing.

"You need a drink, beautiful kiddo," Desmond was saying to her thickly. "Here."

"You know, I'm so morbid," Laura said. "I had a thought: What if cancer were normal, and human life was the anomaly? Isn't that grisly?"

"For God's sake, Laura," Desmond said crossly. Carlos stood up and stretched. "My dear, you're too damned perverse," he said. "*I'm* perverse," Laura said, laughing. "Clara, do you hear that old bum! The thought came to me in a movie theater yesterday. In the dark with all those bodies . . . I could smell someone's dirty feet—"

"That must have been me," Carlos said, and Desmond roared with laughter, calling out, "Carlos! Oh Carlos!" tossing a drink into his open mouth, gulping it down, as everyone joined in until the room rang with the sound. Desmond's lapels were wet with spilled bourbon. His suit, Clara judged, was expensive. By a hair's breadth, Desmond had inherited a family business. That had been Laura's doing. Old Mrs. Clapper had wanted to leave it to Desmond's ex-wife and his daughter. She had been enraged by his marriage to Laura.

"But I won her over," Laura had told Clara once. "I took care of that wicked old woman when she was dying," she'd said. "Oh, I know, Clara, what you're thinking. That I couldn't take care of a flea," and Clara had shaken her head vigorously. "No, no, I wasn't thinking that at all," because Laura had been very drunk, and God knows what she might have said if Clara had agreed with her. "I used to carry those rich bones into the bathroom and lift up her skirt and put her on the toilet," Laura had gone on. "And do you know—in the end—she told me I'd made a man out of her son! And she changed her will. I couldn't stand not having money anymore, for the rest of my life, the way it'd been with Ed, depending only on windfalls from his work. We were so *broke* in so many places, like gypsies. . . ."

Laura's stories. She related them with a strange shallowness, an air of wry disbelief. "But you were good to her," Clara had said, despising herself. "You took care of her." And Laura, with such a knowing look, had replied, "No, no. I knew what I was doing," meeting Clara's effort to excuse her opportunism with no interest. Why, Clara had wondered, did she try? Why did she try to offer absolution to her intransigent mother? Laura recounted her frightful tales as if she were describing a typhoon, and Clara, insistently trying to provide her with the bolt-holes through which people escaped from the moral responsibility for what they did, felt like a fool.

"Damn!" exclaimed Laura, "I forgot to dilute that batch of sleeping pills I brought for Peter."

"How do you do that?" asked Clara.

"The weakest prescription is too strong for him," explained her mother. "I open the capsules, spill out half the contents and fit them back together. Desmond says I look like a witch over a cauldron. Poor old Peter."

At that moment there was a knock at the door and Laura got vigorously to her feet. Desmond said, "I'll go." Then, from the other side of the door came a sustained cry that grew louder every second until it fragmented into shrill, birdlike shrieks. Laura fell back on the bed, laughing wildly and rubbing her face with her hands, this fierce scouring of flesh a habit she shared with Carlos. "He has perfected his seagull cry," Laura gasped. "My God!" exclaimed Carlos. Desmond opened the door and Peter Rice stepped into the room.

He was a few years younger than Laura, although he didn't look it. His thin hair was gray, his features narrow, and from behind his glasses, his pale blue eyes gazed out mildly. He gave an impression of being clean and dry as though he'd been pressed between two large blotters which had absorbed all his vital juices.

He went directly to Laura and she stood up and put her arms around him and for a moment he rested his head on her shoulder. Carlos held up his liquor glass and stared at it thoughtfully. Clara's and Desmond's glances met, then each turned away as though embarrassed. Peter Rice and Laura broke apart gracefully.

"Isn't it marvelous!" said Peter in a gentle, cultivated voice. "It's taken me three years. My masterpiece. I think I've caught it exactly. It's flying from one piling to another. My gull announces the advent of twilight . . . on the cruisers in the marina, people are preparing their suppers of stale carrot sticks and peanuts and hamburgers. They are still wearing their boat gear. Some are drinking from bottles of prepared Manhattans. Some are walking along the pier looking for a small, jolly party they can join. There is the smell of bilge tanks, of roasting meat, of the salt water . . ." And once again, eyes closed, he did his seagull.

Laura laughed until tears came to her eyes. "Charming," murmured Carlos several times. He had, indeed, caught that note of wild complaint in a seagull's cry, thought Clara, and was suddenly miserable. She resolved to make no comment, to remain calm. The main thing was to get through this evening. The Clappers would be gone for months. She would not be compelled to think about Laura, especially if she made a few visits to her grandmother. Her own life was far distant from this hotel room. She must, as she had done as a child, take in good faith what was given. She had not been placed in the wrong crib. Everyone had trouble. She presented the room with a brave face.

"Darling Peter!" Laura said, wiping her eyes with a handkerchief Desmond had handed her. "What will you have?"

"Oh, anything," replied Peter. "Why, this is Clara, isn't it? I haven't seen you for years. What a lovely dress!"

"Yes, isn't it," agreed Laura. "Look, Peter, what Desmond did. He bought me all these clothes . . . on his own."

"Splendid," said Peter.

"Clara, isn't that a French dress?" Laura asked her suddenly.

"No," replied Clara at once. But it was. In another month, she would have paid for it. "I got it on sale," she said.

Desmond said, "You look fine in anything."

"Oh, did you make that reservation for us at *Le Canard Privé*?" Laura asked him.

Peter sipped at his drink. "I've been longing for this," he said. Then he handed Laura a package. "A few things to keep you from being seasick—or to make you seasick."

Laura made a joke of unwrapping the package, uttering

greedy cries, and tearing at the paper until she extracted a half dozen books.

"Oh, Peter, aren't you a dear," she said. "Scandal and mystery stories! My meat!"

"My girl, I even included two we didn't publish," said Peter.

"I did make the reservation this morning, Laura," Desmond declared. "You were standing next to me."

Clara heard Carlos sigh. He was looking at her. "Let's go have another drink by ourselves," he whispered, bending over her. She held his hand and they walked to the table near the windows where the liquor was.

"My dear puppy, I wasn't listening," Laura was saying. "You mustn't be belligerent. I don't listen to your phone conversations. I only wanted to be sure you'd made the reservations."

She should have brought a gift, too, Clara thought. But Carlos hadn't brought anything either, not that he ever did. She could have bought some flowers in the lobby.

"Stop tormenting your poor husband and pay attention to me," demanded Peter. Clara glanced back at them. Laura was rolling her eyes upward with comic exaggeration. Desmond, swaying ever so slightly, stood next to her. Laura touched Peter's cheek lightly with a finger, and Clara saw him blench. But Laura appeared not to notice. "Vel? So vat's new?" she asked, smiling.

Carlos squeezed Clara's arm and nodded at the window. They stood close to it, breathing the rusty-smelling heat from the radiator nearby, not speaking at once, both staring out at the rain, the black sky with its pale underbelly of reflected light, until, persuaded perhaps by the continuing chatter of the other three that he and Clara would not be overheard, Carlos began to speak about Ed Hansen. Ed was their serious subject, delivering them from further displays of affection, allowing their facial muscles, exhausted by nugatory smiles, to relax into sobriety.

"Ed was in town 'Saturday. God. God. I don't know what to do. He wants me to go to Norway with him. He was so damned drunk—after two or three glasses of beer—I didn't know what to do with him. He says Adelaide hates him—Norway! Last year it was the Canary Islands. He's sick. He says Adelaide finds him repulsive . . . he only speaks of the past now . . . always comes to me—"

"Is he really so sick, medically, I mean?" Clara asked. "He told me it was angina, but I don't know when to believe him—I thought you told Laura you hadn't seen him for months?"

"My dear Clarita, your mother—it's a matter of tact—if I told her I'd seen him only a few days ago, she'd become *avid*, want to know everything. She's rather primitive about time. If it's months ago, you see, it's something that may not even have happened."

A faint smile had accompanied his words. Now it faded, leaving behind it his usual expression, one of sad pensiveness. She saw her father lost. He would get nothing from Carlos, not rescue, not even a moment's comfort. "I tried to make him eat something . . ." Carlos said in melancholy accents.

But he wouldn't, Clara guessed, have tried to stop Ed from drinking. She had spent a few afternoons with the two men in Carlos's dark, foul apartment, drinking more than she could tolerate as her father's moods shifted from hilarity to despair and the air grew acrid with smoke, the atmosphere charged with Carlos's helpless irritation. She'd gone because she could not resist a chance to see Ed, even though she knew the hours would be mutilated, debauched. Once, he had sprawled on the dirty couch, nearly insensible, crooning, coughing, retching. "I will catch a great fish, a red salmon, icy its dying flesh," he had cried thickly. "I will take it to my lair in the hills and will place around my neck the chain she has left for me, and eat my fish—"

"For Christ's sake!" Carlos had erupted.

"Ah—you're both against me," Ed had muttered. "I can't help that, my dears, my kittens, my babes. I know you both, your tricks . . ." and then he had begun to bark like a dog.

Staggering beneath his drunken weight, they'd managed to get him into the bedroom. "Ow! Ow! Ow!" he had yipped, his eyes clamped shut, his thin hands clenched against the gray pillowcase.

But there had been other times when she had given in to the thrall of the long friendship between the two men, the charm of their special language with each other, its mysterious allusions, the sense she had, although it bewildered her, of some surviving unimpaired worth each held for the other. Ed did not always drink until he lost consciousness. She had come upon them once in the unchanging dusk of Carlos's living room speaking in low voices. "You must be patient, Ed," Carlos had said gently, again and again. "Husband your strength . . . work at your painting with modesty, no? Isn't that the way, old friend?" as her father—for once—in unemphatic, despairing recital, spoke of his inability to take hold of his life, of this shapeless drift toward annihilation from which he saw no turning. It was too late for everything. Why did women

hate him so? Why couldn't he work anymore, even at photography? He had been a better than competent photographer in his time. He had provided for Laura and himself,
not well but with some style. Why were his nights so tormented by the past that he lay awake grinding his teeth,
groaning with regret, with shame?

They had barely acknowledged her presence, as though
she'd been one of Carlos's young men whom she sometimes found there with them, who smoked idly while he
looked over some of Carlos's old music reviews, or, if he
was musical, allowed his fingers to drift over the keys of
the piano. She had felt as though the two of them were
disappearing before her eyes, fragment of flesh by fragment of bone, replaced by the deepening dark of the evening outside. Days later, recalling that afternoon, she had
known they'd been frightened, the two aging men, unable
to turn on a light.

"I don't know what to tell you," Clara said now to her
uncle. "The last time I saw him—he took me to lunch that
time, which never happened before—and I thought he was
sober, almost. But he wasn't."

Ed had walked with her to her bus stop. He'd been voluble, even brisk, but as the bus drew away from the corner,
she'd looked back at him. He had sagged against the soot-
blackened wall of an old public school, his hat pulled forward over his forehead, his arms hanging lifelessly at his
sides.

There was a shout of laughter from behind them. Clara
turned to see Peter Rice bent over, her mother glittering
with triumphant amusement, Desmond grinning. Laura
must have told a joke.

Clara walked toward them. There was nothing more to

say to Carlos. They had had such conversations before
about Ed. On a bedside table, she noticed a cartoon
clipped from some magazine. She picked it up, then held it
toward Laura. "Did grandma send this?" she asked, knowing Alma's habit of sending cartoons to her children; she'd
been doing it ever since Clara could remember. When
Laura had still been married to Ed and lived in foreign
places, during the months Carlos spent abroad, or when
Eugenio's tourist agency required him to go to California
or New Mexico, their mother would send them, by airmail,
a drawing from a magazine or newspaper, laughing to herself as she clipped out these cartoons, sent them winging
to her scattered children, smiling, perhaps at the thought
of their answering laughter which would anneal the distance, remind them of her existence, appease their irritation at her for reminding them.

"Put that down!"

There was such ferocity in Laura's voice that Clara
dropped the piece of paper. It floated just beneath the bed,
and Carlos, arrested by Laura's cry, let a match burn down
to his fingers. In the silence—everyone was silent—Clara
saw that a stem was missing from the eyeglasses Carlos
was wearing.

"I'm sorry," Clara said lamely. Peter Rice retrieved the
cartoon and put it back carefully on the table. Then Laura
shook her head as though confused. "Oh—I don't know
what's the matter with me. . . . Of course, look at it,
Clara. Here, take it!" And then she grabbed her brother's
arm. "Carlos!" all mock severity now, "Get those damned
specs fixed! Shame on you!"

"They're fine," he said mildly.

"Why, Carlos, they aren't yours! Look, Laura, they don't
even fit him," said Desmond.

"Someone left them at my apartment," Carlos said rue-
fully, reminding them all of his reputation as the laziest
man in the world. He smiled winsomely.

There was a story Ed Hansen told, of how when he and
Carlos had gone on a brief trip to Mexico, Carlos had said,
on their first evening in Taxco, that he didn't feel like
arranging for rooms with the hotel manager. Would Ed
mind getting a translator? And during the subsequent
dealing with the manager, while a young Mexican boy
grabbed off the street translated for Ed, Carlos had sat
in a chair, nodding, Ed reported, in voluptuous weariness,
as though a young pupil was reciting an often repeated
lesson for an old master.

Waking at a late hour of a Sunday morning, knowing he
ought to visit his mother at the home, knowing that he
would not, aware of the noxious stink of his apartment, of
stale food and dust and unwashed sheets, Carlos would
fold his hands behind his head and lie there, tears running
down his cheeks, thinking of his used-up life, of lovers
dead or gone, of investments made unwisely, of his violent
sister who might telephone him at any minute and, with
her elaborate killer's manners, in her beautiful deep voice,
make some outrageous demand upon him, making clear
she knew not only the open secrets of his life but the hidden ones, knew about his real shiftlessness, his increasing
boredom with sexual pursuit, his unappeased sexual longing, his terror of age. "I'm becoming an old sow," he would
whisper to himself, trying to keep at bay the thought of his
mother waiting in the disinfectant, linoleum-smelling
stillness of the old people's home for him to come and see
her.

"I'm really going to have my prescription filled one of
these days," he said to Laura.

"Oh, Carlos . . ." Laura shook her head with mock despair.

"You might get a seeing eye dog," suggested Peter.

"Oh, Peter, then he'd have to *feed* it, and take it out—"

"Not necessarily," Carlos said, and laughed, as did everyone, and new drinks were made. Laura raised hers to the group. "Gosh, it's so damned nice to have you all here! Carlos! Clarita! You're really here. Isn't it, Desmond? Doesn't it feel delicious?"

"Oh yes . . . it's wonderful," Desmond replied. His face was inflamed, his eyes were dulled.

"The restaurant Desmond found has the most marvelous eggs *à la Russe,*" Laura said animatedly. "Isn't that your favorite, Clara? Aren't you the great mayonnaise and eggs lover?"

"Oh, God! I'm smoking a cigarette and now I've lit another one," exclaimed Peter.

"No seagull would do such a dreadful thing," Laura smiled. Peter looked like a bashful youth unexpectedly caressed. "I know some very low-class seagulls," he said. "Now, let's see your dresses, darling, or, as my mother used to call them, frocks."

Desmond, after glancing quickly at his wife, touched Clara's arm. "How's tricks? Really, I mean," he said.

"I think I'll get another ice cube," she said, thinking, it's his turn with me now. At the drinks table, Desmond grabbed up an ice cube in his large hand which was, Clara thought, unusually hairy—as though he was wearing a mitt. "Laura said you'd found a pretty good job."

"Well, it's an *awful* good job—but, there are nice people there," she didn't want to be caught complaining. "When I turned in my first expense account sheet, the executives

all came to see me. I have a tiny office, and the six of them
crowded in. It was quite funny. I'd turned in this expense
sheet for $6.75, and they asked me, was I trying to make
them look like crooks?"

Desmond snorted and rocked toward her on his heels;
did he imagine he looked shrewd, pursing up his lips and
scowling importantly?

"I'm sure they explained," he said.

"Well, I had just put down bus and subway fares, you
see—" but Desmond was gone; with three unsteady steps
he had moved to the bed where Laura was reclining.
"Darling? Do you want more ice?"

Clara was used to not finishing sentences. Her thoughts
returned at once to a nettled, uneasy speculation about the
cartoon her mother had at first charged her not to touch,
but it was a futile exercise. In no other company more
than among these Spaniards was Clara so conscious of a
discrepancy between surface talk and inner preoccupation.
They sped from one posture to another, eliciting with
amused cries each other's biases, pretending to discover
anew the odd notions each harbored, amusing themselves
nearly to death! Until Laura, with a hard question, thrust a
real sword through the paper props, and there would be for
a second, a minute, the startled mortified silence of people
caught out in a duplicity for which they could find no explanation. Then, with what indulgence, what tenderness,
Laura rescued them, sometimes.

I will simply pick up that cartoon from the table, Clara
told herself, looking at a small pool of water that had
leaked through the window. She turned toward the bedside table. Between her and it was a matched luggage set.
It was new and looked expensive. She would have to get

around the other side of the bed where Peter Rice and Carlos were standing with their drinks. But what the hell did she care about the cartoon?

"Come over here . . . don't be so exclusive, Miss," her mother called.

"Beautiful suitcases," said Clara.

"Our new line," boasted Desmond.

The luggage had cost the Clappers nothing. The inheritance which Laura had secured them was a fine leather business. The sales were handled by representatives in all the major cities of the country. "Very refeened," Laura would say, grinning. One profitable year, they had bought a farm in Pennsylvania, and there they lived, making an occasional trip to New York or, more infrequently, a journey abroad.

As Clara carefully avoided the luggage in her passage from window to chair, where she sat down, she thought Laura's smile was touched with melancholy. She seemed, for the moment, to be at rest, a kind of sated rest, Clara reflected. The room was so close; perhaps we are slowly suffocating—the air seemed composed of the very stuff of the beige carpeting. Suddenly the radiator emitted a noisy sustained hiss of steam. A new Vesuvius, Clara thought— we'll be found, later, as we are at this moment, stiffened in our chains like the dog of Pompeii.

"This hotel has gone downhill," Desmond said querulously.

"Not to spite you, Desmond," remarked Laura.

"I didn't say—"

"Clara! Look out! He's going to spill his drink on you!"

Clara reared up in her chair. But Desmond was standing several feet away from her. He looked dumfounded, held his drink up to eye level, mumbled, "Christ! It's nearly empty." Peter Rice spoke hurriedly. "Laura, listen. You must see the Blue People."

"Peter Rice!" Laura exclaimed, her eyes enormous, glittering. "You are, to put it mildly, somewhat forgetful. Do you know how many times you've told us about those Blue People of yours! Good God! What happened to you in those Berber tents?"

"I've never told you about the Blue People."

"But you did!"

"I never heard about them," claimed Desmond with eerie clarity, a falsetto sharpness of enunciation, as though a sober ventriloquist had taken charge of his voice.

"I haven't either," said Carlos.

A minor impasse, a trivial lapse in someone's memory— it happened in conversation often enough. But not to be followed by such a stony silence as this. They had all been stopped cold. On Peter Rice's face, Clara saw a reflection of her own malaise. Carlos had gone blank. Desmond swayed as though his balance was giving way.

Yet Laura could be contradicted. Clara had seen her charmed by disputation, bend upon it the playful intensity she gave to riddles and puzzles. Why was she staring at the wall with such a tragic look? Her limbs stiff as though convulsed? What had happened now?

The guests had gathered to bid the travelers farewell. They had managed to keep things going—the trip, Carlos's laziness, bird imitations, Clara's looks—prodding and pulling words out of themselves as though urging a sluggish beast into its cage, and now it was out, this beast, menacing them with a suddenly awakened appetite. What meat would satisfy it? Clara imagined herself uttering a groan, a loud exclamation. But not at family gatherings any more than on ordinary social occasions did people burst forth into the mad, disconnected fragments of speech that might hold some tenuous consonance with what they were really thinking, feeling.

Desmond, in slow motion, stumbled toward the bathroom. Then Peter, with an uneasy smile, spoke. "Well, dearie, if you've heard it all before, what *haven't* you heard before? We all repeat stories about what we've loved or hated—"

Laura suddenly turned to them. She was smiling. Carlos began, very meditatively, to unwrap the cellophane from a cigar. Clara heard her own sigh and hoped no one else had.

"I was going to say," Peter went on, "that I saw the wickedest dance anyone ever dreamed up done by a little, thin girl of fourteen. On her knees, mind you, using her arms and shoulders—"

"Some poor child whore!" Clara interrupted shrilly, "forced to her knees by disgusting, primitive—" and then startled by her own outburst, she fell silent.

"Now, Clara," said her mother tolerantly, "none of that talk. Nobody forces people to their knees except themselves. . . ."

Peter was looking at Clara with surprise. He had thought her a muted, oppressed young woman. As Laura's daughter, what else could she have been? But the indignation he had heard in her voice, the faint glitter of hysteria—still, these reserved, brooding people were prone to take unconsidered swings at anything. They were like recluses who mistake a footfall for an invading army.

"Were you in Rabat?" Carlos asked politely.

"You must have been in your nappies!" exclaimed
Laura. "It was just before the war, wasn't it, Peter?"

"Yes. I was in Rabat. And I was twenty, Laura, old
enough. But primitive, Clara . . . I went to Quito last year
during my vacation. An Indian girl used to come to do my
laundry. That Jivaro profile of hers . . . I used to watch
her iron my shirts. I loved her face. She would turn suddenly, and smile at me. The most radiant smile I ever saw!
The men of her tribe had probably smiled at the mis-
sionaries like that before they hacked them up with ma-
chetes. And in Haiti, in Morocco, I've seen that sacred
smile, ineffable, the way we must all have smiled once—"

"For God's sake! What crap!" erupted Desmond crossly.
He was standing next to the bathroom door, staring at the
bottle of bourbon on the table. Had he already finished off
half of it? But no one paid him any attention. They were
watching Clara, who had risen to her feet. She was strug-
gling to control a profound agitation; her lips trembled, she
blinked, she gripped one hand with the other. Carlos hid
himself in a great puff of cigar smoke.

"Sacred, ineffable, tum-te-tum-te-tum," mocked Laura
loudly. "Do you like my smile, Peter? I'm a primitive."

Clara spoke, her voice tremulous. "What about the creatures that slink around this city, who kill without a flicker
of pity? They smile too. Is that what you mean?"

"How would you know, kiddo?" asked Desmond.

Peter took hold of Clara's hand. It was damp. Gradually,
the fingers he was holding closed around his own. "I didn't
mean not human," he said. "Really, I had something else
in mind. Innocence . . . before the fall, all that. . . ."

He was very faintly repelled by the closeness, the in-
tertwining of their fingers, their palms lightly sweating

one against the other. Yet how unconsciously, how touch-
ingly her hand had curled around his! But that was
enough. He let go of her and stepped away. What had he
roused up in her with his "primitive smile" routine? He
was so used to his own set pieces that he didn't even
bother to listen to himself anymore. But this time, he'd
done it. The girl looked on the verge of tears. He had simply been keeping the conversation moving along. He
glanced quickly at Laura. And all at once it was borne in
upon him powerfully that she was really the girl's mother,
that there was something here he had not known about
before, had never speculated about, something singular.

"You're so passionate," murmured Laura to Clara. She
swung her legs off the bed, and the box of dresses tumbled
to the floor. Clara went to pick them up, and as she replaced them on the foot of the bed, her mother gave her a
broad, rather lewd, wink. Clara laughed and said impul-
sively, gratefully, "What pretty dresses they are!"

Grinning, her mother fiddled with her sapphire ring
then, suddenly, her hand shot out and she grasped the
hem of Clara's dress and turned it up. Sewn to the seam
was a small white silk tag on which was printed the name,
Christian Dior. Clara stood frozen as Laura's fingers gradually released the cloth of her dress. What reasons would
ever prevail against the implacable judgment she saw on
Laura's face, which was slowly, slowly turning from her to
Peter Rice?

"More drinks, all? Anyone?" Desmond was holding up a
bottle. "Out of ice, darling. Shall I phone for more?" But
no one answered him, and he was not surprised. He
smiled to himself. He didn't give a good goddamn for ice,
for bored old Carlos sulking near the window like a moth-

eaten bear, clutching his cigar—that sack of Spanish guts
. . . dirty, lazy old queen. Christ! Didn't he know there
was a glob of chewing gum stuck to one of his shoes? If
they *were* his shoes. You'd think he sold pencils in Times
Square. Desmond didn't give a goddamn, either, for all
that frenzied jabbering going on between Laura and Peter
Rice.

He laughed aloud to think of what Laura would say
about them all once they were gone, once she was alone
with him, when he wouldn't have to worry about what she
was thinking, of how she was being reminded of the years
before. As if he didn't know that they talked about Ed
Hansen the second he, Desmond, was out of sight! What
else was there for them to talk about?

Desmond had met Laura and Ed in Paris years ago, and
he'd been dazzled by Ed at first, just like any other fool.
Ed had just punched a Frenchman because Laura had
said the man looked at her salaciously while the three of
them were slowly rising in one of those hotel cage elevators, and he'd thought he would go out of his mind with
laughter at Ed's description of what had happened. "Hit
him!" Laura had demanded, and Ed had! And then had
picked the poor dazed son of a bitch up from the floor, and
dragged him out into a corridor and covered him with
some soiled sheets a chambermaid had left in a cart—so
he wouldn't catch his death of cold, Ed had said. That was
when Laura was in her late thirties, and Desmond had
thought she looked like a slightly bruised dahlia. And Marjorie, his own wife, hadn't had the slightest idea of how
stirred he'd been by Laura, wild to take her to bed, to have
her all for himself, to watch her forever, to track down and
discover what it was in her nature that led her to such

thrilling displays of temperament, those scenes that had so disgusted Marjorie, that had so exhilarated him. Later, Laura had told him that Ed had known all along that Desmond was mad to get her, and how he'd laughed at Desmond. Desmond knew they'd both laughed. He'd never forgive them that.

He'd known, too, they had a child somewhere, living with the grandmother in Cuba, known the child wouldn't be a problem for him. Laura wasn't anybody's mother. Not like Marjorie, clamping her jaw shut, buttoning up Ellen's jacket, saying, "I don't want my child within a thousand miles of that Spanish bitch!" And that hadn't been much of a problem either. He felt in his pocket suddenly. Where the hell had he put Ellen's letter? He always answered her letters. Laura didn't know that. He usually managed to get to the mail before she did, but he'd slipped up this time. He'd send the girl a postcard from Rabat. He might even speak to Peter privately about helping her get a job in publishing. He supposed she had ambitions—silly illusions about literature—an ordinary lawyer's office not being up to Marjorie's expectations for "my child!" Desmond said aloud, "Damned right!"

"I'm sorry, what did you say?" Clara had come over to him and was looking distractedly at the ice bucket, the bottles.

"Oh, you know . . ." Desmond said thickly, "the ice . . . they never bring enough of it . . . damned hotels."

Clara poured some scotch into her glass. "I don't care about ice."

"That's right."

"Your ship must be getting all wet in this rain—the decks, the portholes blurred. When it rains like this, I get

the feeling that travel is an illusion. Do you know what I
mean?"

"Oh, now . . ."

"It's hard to imagine there's a place where it isn't raining, do you see?"

I am the only sensible person in this place, he thought,
and frowned at her, as though to bring her to her senses.
What was she looking so apologetic about? Then, abruptly,
Clara left him. Had he told her to shut up? He'd thought
it, but God! had he said it?

The cartoon Clara had gone to look for had disappeared
from the bedside table. Had Laura chewed it up and swallowed it? If it had been there, she could have remarked
upon it and so begun a new conversation with her mother,
one that would release her, for the moment, from the mortification of her lie about the dress. Her squalid lie; the
peculiar look of prophecy on her mother's face, what was
she to make of it?

Her dress was hot against her skin. Peter Rice glanced
at her; an impersonal smile touched his lips. She felt she
was about to faint, to fall, not from drink or from the
warmth of the room, but from a powerful recollection that
swept over her so that she seemed to feel the flesh, the
limbs, of her lover, Harry Dana, pressing her down, holding her down, the hateful dress abandoned in the corner
where she'd dropped it.

She was suddenly aware of a curious odor. It was, she
recalled, that hair treatment her mother used, a kind of tar
to rid herself of some minor scalp trouble. She had not
realized until that instant that she must have been moving
closer and closer to Laura. What an awful haircut she'd
gotten herself! Clara sniffed discreetly. There it was again,

a black, marshy smell, a touch of petroleum, an ancient ooze, the true elements of that Spanish blood, *sangre pura,* not a scalp treatment at all! Pure blood! The Spaniards had consumed whole populations of Indians, of Arabs, of black Moors, of Jews. God, how she would like to have been present when her father had said to Laura, "You know, of course, that you're Sephardic, my queen, don't you?" At least, so he had told Clara, swearing he'd said it. And he'd shown Clara a little tintype he had stolen from Laura, a photograph of Laura's father, her own grandfather long dead before she'd been born, a handsome, swarthy, small man dressed in gypsy costume for the sitting, a swaggering, sporty little cock in a rakish caballero hat. "From Cadiz," Ed had said, "never to be mentioned in front of your Uncle Eugenio!"

As if she would have mentioned anything to Uncle Eugenio, his own father or his own shoelaces! For there was a man whom "pure blood" had driven crazy, who carried, rolled up in his pocket, photocopies of pages of coats of arms he'd found in genealogical encyclopedias in the library. It was said that Eugenio never touched anyone's hand—fear of contamination, perhaps. Once, when he'd stayed at Alma's old apartment, sleeping on the studio couch among the rattletrap furnishings of the living room, Clara had heard him scream in the middle of the night like a horse pitched onto barbed wire. And once he had kicked a hole in the plaster of the wall, waking to find his foot covered with blood. Alma had pasted over the hole a picture of an ape she had found in a copy of *Life* magazine.

"For God's sake! The dresses are falling again! Put them away, will you, Laura?" Desmond said irritably. Laura made a comic face and grinned. Her good humor was holding, Clara assured herself as Laura hung the dresses in a closet. Each passing moment was bringing them all closer to the safety of the restaurant. As Laura had re-marked about herself, she didn't misbehave in public the way she used to in the old days.

"What are you doing, Clara? Did I hear you mention public relations?" Peter inquired.

"That shit!" exploded Desmond. Then, his eyes on his wife, he said, as though in apology, "Well, everybody knows it's—"

Laura covered her eyes with the palms of her hands. "What everybody knows," she intoned dramatically, "is that my husband is tipsy, having provided himself with a few little extras over there in his corner." Her hands flew away; her eyes sparkled; her amiability distracted them from the steaming expletive, the intrusive pure ugliness of it. Saved although from what, Clara couldn't think—they looked at her expectantly. "Tell us about it, Clara," Laura said.

She told them what she thought would amuse them, but kept herself out of it. She feared, without knowing why, that the weight of one word of personal feeling would sink them all. And her throat tightened at Carlos's faint sigh, when she saw her mother gazing fixedly at her own hands and Peter Rice staring blankly at a telephone directory. She described the agency code system for client meetings where account executives alerted each other to uncon-scious personal habits by one or two or three discreet raps on the conference table. "We have a scratcher in the of-fice," she said. "But when he hears three raps, he jumps like a stung rabbit and folds his hands."

They did laugh then, all except Desmond. He didn't care

what they were going on about now. Had he made that
reservation at the restaurant? It was one thing he prided
himself on, his efficiency in making arrangements. He
looked at Laura; she was very handsome, sitting there on
the bed. Handsome, heavy, wanton, he thought half-
dreaming—like some large animal bogged down in its own
heat and weight.

"'Time is ever fleeting,'" sang Peter Rice. "What on
earth? Where did that come from? Clara, you've described
your agency perfectly. Appalling. Are you interested in
publishing? It's not much better but its style is somewhat
more—" and he shrugged and lit a cigarette.

Like a large animal, crooned Desmond to himself, in a
fen, its hide muddied, matted, beshitted, the rank smell of
dead leaves—

"Desmond?" his name, so softly spoken, nearly a whisper. He felt a sharp pain in his bowels. Laura could not
possibly know what he'd been thinking, yet it came to him
that she knew *something* about him, this minute, which, if
she chose to reveal it, would mortify him. He knew that
flat-eyed look of hers, that whisper! He poured a large
drink into his glass and held it up so she could damn well
see it. He deserved better after Marjorie, after those years
with her and that child, Ellen, Ellen Clapper, writing him
stupid letters—Laura saw how stupid. Then he understood! All that Laura knew was that he had, perhaps,
taken a bit too much to drink.

"Desmond. What time is the reservation for?"

"Seven-thirty," he said. How small everyone's head
looked! He shook his own head to clear his vision. But it
wouldn't come right.

"You didn't!"

"Well—what's wrong, for God's sake. . . ."

"But, my dear! Dan is calling then, about Lucy, to tell us how she is!"

"Why don't you call Dan, then?"

"It would insult him. He'd think I didn't trust him."

"Who's Lucy?" asked Carlos with a look of distaste; it would be disagreeable if his sister and her husband started quarreling now, with so many hours still to be endured.

"Their dog," whispered Clara. "That old terrier."

"I thought Dan was the dog," Carlos said.

"Listen, if he calls on time—it'll only take a second. And we don't have to be in the restaurant on the dot," protested Desmond.

Laura looked at him affectionately. "Old muddled brains," she said, smiling.

"The thing about being in publishing," began Peter, "is that you must seem to be interested in art but imprisoned in a system that only values money. The superior *chic*, of course, is to appear interested only in money."

"How disgusting," said Carlos languidly.

"The dog is all right!" Desmond suddenly shouted. "I don't see what's wrong with the reservation." He fell silent, then looked truculently at Peter. "What are you carrying on about?" he asked gruffly. "So what else is new about American publishing? About *artistes* and their old nannies?"

Laura jumped off the bed and walked over to her husband. "What dog, darling? That was hours ago. . . . Have you been drinking a little?" She pinched his chin and turned to wink at the others as though to invite them to share the joke. Everyone was aware that Desmond had called Peter Rice an old nanny. Clara, ashamed of the relief she felt at not being the cause of the somber, thorny silence which followed Laura's words, watched Peter covertly. His eyes were cast down, his hands clasped. He glanced up at her. "Culture makes one bitter," he said in such a low voice she wasn't sure she'd heard him right.

Now Laura was speaking rapidly but inaudibly to Desmond, in whose expression petulance warred with a peculiar gratification. "I won't. I'll stop," he suddenly said clearly. Laura turned to the others. "Are you all starving?"

Clara asserted quickly that she was not. "I'm going to *be* starving any minute," said Carlos. But Peter was silent. He lifted up a plastic-covered card from the table. "The hotel has its own jeweler," he said.

"An vy not?" asked Laura with what she apparently imagined was a Jewish accent. Clara started guiltily as though she'd been caught out by all the Jews she knew consorting with this anti-Semite.

"I have to order up my diamonds," Laura cried. "After all, I trow avay my old vones!"

"That old joke . . ." said Peter. "I'm ashamed of you, Laura."

"Well, my dear, my daughter doesn't bring me any new ones anymore."

Clara winced. She and Alma, dropping their jokes and cartoons over the rim of the volcano, seemed alike in their similar persuasion that this woman, this link between them, must be propitiated, that she was not a point in a continuing line of human descent but the apex of a triangle. Her heart beat painfully—it was not that she had ever given much thought to having children, but she felt as though she'd suddenly gotten news that she couldn't have any, that the geometric fancy which had taken hold of her imagination—she could see the iron triangle as clearly as she could see the hotel telephone—was the shape of her fate.

But how did Laura behave with Alma? She couldn't recall much from the few times she had seen them together. They spoke Spanish. Clara, who had always addressed her mother as Laura, had been oddly thrilled to hear Laura say, "Mamá." She had observed how, in those scattered encounters among the years of absence, Laura had shown toward her mother an almost commanding protectiveness, and when Alma's sighs and exclamations of pleasure began gradually to subside, and after a brief interlude during which the old woman gave her daughter news of her life, extracting from her money-troubled days the little sidelights she thought would appeal to Laura's sense of irony, might even evoke her admiration for Alma's high spirits in dreary circumstances, the pretend life would suddenly collapse. Tears streaming down her face, she would cry out that she had been *"abandonada"* by everyone, resisting all effort to comfort her until that point when Laura seized her hands and said, "Now, Mamá. We'll have no more of this!" Alma, the old child of her own daughter, would smile again, somewhat piteously. . . . Sometimes, Laura had left a few dollars in her hands. She had "swiped" them from Ed, she would say. When she left—no one knew when she would reappear—there would be between the grandmother and her granddaughter a shocked, bereaved silence as though someone had died.

Both Alma and Clara, like foreigners who practice a new language, especially its idioms, had adopted Laura's characterization of the Hansens' nearly unchanging financial state. It was called being "broke." The child Clara sensed in that word its inherent promise: Being broke was a condition subject to sudden dramatic reversal. That the reversal never came, that year after year, coming home from school and hanging up her threadbare winter coat in the closet, she could see her grandmother's one pair of "good" shoes grow shabbier and shabbier, could not dislodge from her mind the thrilling expectation that money would come, that there would be a great festival of money. But, in the midst of her life, Clara knew they were poor, among the poorest in their corner of Brooklyn. Yet she was haunted by that contrary possibility, that they were only "broke," that rescue was on the way—always on the way.

Alma had had an income, although very small, from relatives in Cuba, and Carlos contributed a few dollars now and then. Otherwise, how would they have lived?

"I don't hear jokes anymore," she said to Laura, but her voice cracked suddenly with an effort to conceal a spurt of anger. "Broke!" she wanted to shout, "you sons of bitches, what do you know?"

She was frightened. She got up and walked over to the window. What was the matter with her? What would be the use of breaking off her tenuous connection with Laura now? Nothing to be gained; nothing, even, to be lost. She was no longer at the mercy of adults. She was one herself, buying her own clothes, paying her own rent. It was Alma who was still dependent on Laura's mercy—whatever that was! She wondered if her grandmother knew that Laura had tried to get city aid to pay for the cost of the home for the elderly? She knew because Laura had told her, describing how the investigators had discovered that Desmond and Carlos and even Eugenio had "resources" which canceled out any claims they might imagine they had on public money. The woman investigator who had interviewed her had been scandalized, outraged, Laura reported without embarrassment or comment. Laura had merely observed that Carlos and Eugenio were "bums," and that she couldn't see how she could ask Desmond to carry their responsibility. But in the end, she had asked Desmond and he had agreed to provide the larger share of the money, and so, she had told Clara, each month they spent a fortune on telephone calls trying to hound the two brothers to pay something, anything, toward Alma's expenses.

Oh God! Why wouldn't she go and visit her grandmother? Had she inherited that profound spiritual indolence of the Maldonadas?

"Clara must make a new reservation for us, Desmond. Won't you, Clara?"

Her mother was looking at her archly. Clara nodded.

"Ask the operator to get the number for you," Laura directed.

"She doesn't have to call," Desmond protested.

Laura appeared not to have heard him. She was studying her ankles, turning them this way and that. Peter Rice was preoccupied with fitting himself into a small boudoir chair. Desmond's heavy breathing was audible in the silence—he sounded like a horse, a few stalls away, breathing evenly in the blankness of the night.

When Laura looked up, she seemed unaware of Peter's fidgeting, of Carlos brushing cigar ashes from the coverlet of the other bed where he had spilled them. She stared at Desmond as though they were alone. Clara had the startling impression that her mother's eye sockets were empty, were like mouths, opening to scream. The heavy lids dropped suddenly. "If Eugenio were here, that would be all of us," she said to no one in particular.

Conversation began at once, although to Clara's question about how long they would be in Africa, Desmond hesitated so long, she wondered if he knew what she was asking him.

"Why do they always do it?" Peter Rice asked, rubbing the fabric of the chair with one finger.

"Do what?" Laura asked.

"So pretentious, this fabric. Fake brocade, isn't it? Why not be plain? Why not a plain, decent chair? Why is music played in elevators? And what music! And those revolting gold tassels on airline menus, and what are those designs stamped on your bedspreads? Coats of arms, no less! I mean—"

"Peter," Laura said. "Don't waste your nerves on trivia. The world is wrecked, my dears. There's no point at all in being sniffy about the corpse's low taste in winding sheets."

"I was only babbling," Peter said defensively.

"Have you seen my mother recently?" Carlos asked Laura. He had been silent for some time, and now his voice was formal and chilled as though, during that time of silence, he had broken off his connections with everyone in the room. He was already turning away from his sister; his interest in her answer seemed negligible.

"My mother." That is how each of her children referred to Alma. They shut each other out, Clara thought. She hoped the subject of Alma would not engage them for long. Her heart pressed up weakly against her ribs. She felt the imminence of an attack against her. But there was no defense except the confession that she could not bring

herself to visit the old woman. She cast a furtive glance at
Laura.

They were all staring at Laura. She had clasped her
drink to her forehead frantically as though an ache there
must be pressed away. Her eyes were closed. In the tension of her raised arms, the loosened curls tumbling forward, legs lifting toward her stomach, one shoe beginning
to slip from a foot, she was like the personification of ca-
lamity.

Desmond cried out incoherently, Peter stood up, Carlos
backed away toward the windows, and Clara, remembering a glass of whiskey hurled at her by Laura so many
years before she could not recall the place, only the arc of
the glass, crouched in her chair.

The legs came down, the foot found the fallen shoe and
inserted itself, the drink was held out to be appraised by
the now wide-open eyes, and Laura grinned at them like a
rogue.

"Your mother?" she asked lightly of Carlos. "You rascal!
I drove all the way up from the farm last week to see *your
mother,* and you, you wretch, live fifteen minutes from the
home and haven't been for a month. Isn't he a rascal,
Peter? Her very favorite, too! Even—even Eugenio went!
Although I heard he stayed just long enough to taunt her
with the details of some dinner party he crashed into. You
know, Peter, don't you, how Eugenio treats my mother?
When he used to stay at the apartment, months sometimes
when he had no money, he'd tell her about his dinner parties. He can't bear to touch anybody—I suppose you must
have noticed that, Clara—he always stands at least ten feet
away from other human bodies. Isn't it funny he should be
running a travel agency and sending people away all the

time? But I started to say—that he used to torment Mamá about the meals he was served in grand houses, as though it was *her* fault she didn't live in a grand house with servants to take care of him properly!"

Uncle Eugenio had once said to Clara, "My mother was so beautiful when she used to take care of herself." And when Clara was older, though no less ill at ease in Eugenio's presence, he confided to her that it was the childishness in his mother's character, *"fatal* childishness," he had said, that had brought the family so low. Did he, Clara wondered, hold his mother responsible too for the Spanish-American War which had dislodged the Maldonadas' grip on their Cuban holdings? But he never spoke of such things, wars, depressions, the state of the world, seeming as unaware, Clara thought, as her mother and Carlos of the existences beyond the rain-blurred windows which impinged upon their own. Those two, like their brother, were interested in what was singular, aberrant. But was there anybody, she asked herself, who *thought* about the world beyond their own window? Still, there was something distinctive about the Maldonadas' posture of aloofness; it was a quality of contempt.

So Eugenio had been deprived of his right to servants, to privilege, to a fortune, by his impractical mother and some old battles which had left his father's plantation in ashes! And he would tell Clara about the china and fine linen in some old woman's home, laughing crazily in the middle of his enraptured descriptions, for no reason she could comprehend. And he had seemed crazy to her, standing in the meager living room of Alma's apartment where the radiator sent out sprays of hot, dirty water, where the windows looked out at blank walls, where all things were pinched, poor, broken, worn, ragged.

Eugenio knew a number of old ladies whose circumstances reminded him of all that he had lost, and in whose houses his cold sycophancy, his careful foreigner's diction, his elaborate courtliness screened the cupidity, the longing, with which he noted every teacup, every bibelot, every scrap of evidence of the blissful oblivion which money only can bring. His small tourist office became a favorite of rich, elderly travelers. He knew such *refined* places to stay. One poster hung on the wall of his office, a romantic photograph of a castle in Spain. Clara, stopping by once, had looked at it closely. It was a twelfth-century fortress; the mist enveloping it did not conceal its brutality.

There was no photograph of the farmhouse on Long Island Alma had bought with nearly the last of her money when she had first come to the United States from Cuba after her husband's death. The purchase, Eugenio had said, was a catastrophic mistake, largely the fault of Carlos, who always encouraged Alma in her most impulsive actions. How beautiful the meadows had been then, Alma told Clara. Meadows and house were now buried beneath a broad highway. By the time Clara was born, Alma had begun the series of moves from bad to worse apartments which was to end up finally in those two rooms on the edge of Flatbush. Clara had taken her first steps on the graveled roof, had practiced running on the black-and-white tiled floors of the halls which smelled of dirty mops and ammonia, had learned to fear the villainous, creaking elevator whose metal door her grandmother struggled to hold open for her as she darted past it, expecting at any second to be squashed like a cockroach.

In later years, when she went to visit Alma, she could not see how the old woman could still hold back that terrible door, get past it before it slammed shut with a deafening crash, and draw the rusty gate, inside, to its latch. By that time, Alma could not use the stairs; her feet were deformed by huge bunions and corns; she had had to cut holes in her shoes, snipping the cheap leather with nail scissors.

Among Eugenio's old ladies, his mother was the only failure. Clara had reason to remember one of them. Señora Josepha had owned vast properties in Colombia. Her estate was handled by four lawyers who kept her traveling around the world year after year on cruises, or allowed her to rest briefly in luxurious hotels. Clara never met her, but Eugenio must have said something about her to the Señora. She'd been very old when she died alone in a tower suite of the old Ritz. Of course, Eugenio said bitterly, she didn't look old because she'd known how to take care of herself. She wore little veiled silk hats, Eugenio said, smiling as though at the endearing idiosyncrasy of a lover, and she had hard little hands, beautifully manicured. Of course, she used only her own silver whether on a ship or in a hotel. She had left the bulk of her fortune to a Colombian relative, but there had been a few single bequests, one of which was a trunk full of things for Clara.

Eugenio described the trunk, how when its lid was raised, a smell of wealth had filled the air. There had been some clothes from Worth, chiffon embroidered with silver thread, sachets, a small fur wrap, unworn lingerie covered with lace. Laura had taken it. "My sister, that is, your mother, was able to make use of some of the articles. They would not have suited your age."

In fact, Clara had not heard about that trunk until some years later. She had been electrified to learn that her own name had been written down in a legal document by a rich old woman she'd never known. And she'd agreed, at once, with Eugenio that it was unlikely she could have used any of those things, undoubtedly old-fashioned, more fit for a museum; there were hardly occasions in her life for wearing chiffon. So she had rushed past the stolen inheritance, but it had lodged itself in her mind, a large, oblong box with a jammed lock, a lid rusted shut. She'd never get it open. Disappointment gave way, over the years, to a bitter triumph like that people sometimes experience in consistent bad fortune.

Laura was beckoning to her conspiratorially. She went to her.

"Do make the call to the restaurant," she whispered. "If Desmond comes near, pretend you're talking to a friend. He's so foolish when he gets stubborn." Laura smiled, absolving her husband of any *serious* charge. "If we're late, I know we'll lose the table. Do call, Clarita."

Clara got the number of the restaurant. On the telephone, too, she felt the presence of multitudes, heard the faint murmur of other voices pressed against her own like threads in a skein. The French-accented voice at the other end of the line confirmed the Clapper reservation, and interrupted Clara's explanation that they might be a few minutes late with an impatient reassurance that it didn't matter.

If Desmond had come close, she could have pretended she was speaking to Harry Dana, at the moment, she imagined, sitting at the dinner table with his wife and two children. She would have pretended she was someone from Harry's office—an emergency matter, sorry to bother you, Mrs. Dana—she'd never heard his wife's voice or the voices of his children.

Carlos was saying that he wished he were going on a trip, to Agadir, to Dakar, almost any place would do.

"Too busy?" asked Laura dryly. "Too many important matters that need your attention?"

"Exactly!" said Carlos impudently.

"And what for?" Peter Rice asked irritably. "The beautiful old names of those ancient places are all that's left. I can just see you, Carlos, running into an American family studying the mosaics in a former bordello. They'll have the new baby along and a supply of diapers and perhaps the dog and cat. They'll visit each room of the bordello, discuss its furnishings, inform their five-year-olds as to the use of the mirrors and the leather thongs—"

"Oh, shut up . . ." mumbled Desmond.

"Peter!" cried Laura. "How bitchy! What an absolutely terrible old snob you are! Why are you such a cross old seagull tonight? The German tourists are far worse than the Americans. They make twice as much noise. And the French begin to smell something bad as soon as they leave their own borders. Americans are respectful abroad. They have a kind of innocence, you know."

Desmond felt an impulse to polish his shoes, to make them shine, to get down on his knees and strop them as though he were honing a razor, to kick his wife.

What the hell did she know about Americans? A goddamned spic. *Spic,* he said over and over again to himself, all these spics and that boring prig of an editor. Puritan, libertine, there was no difference except in pretense. Laura needed to wash her face. He could feel that she was getting dangerously tense. Who knew her better than he did? Oh, Christ! Why didn't they all go away and leave the two of them alone! Something was up with her; she'd had her hands all over her face—every time he looked at her, she was rubbing her cheeks. He looked at his watch, then brought it close to his eyes. It was getting a lot harder to tell time without glasses. He had a pair but he seldom used them. He supposed his eyes were worse right now because he'd hardly slept a wink last night. That's why he'd had a few drinks more than he supposed he should have had.

All night—had he been awake all night?—he'd been thinking of his own death. In twenty years, he'd be seventy, nearly seventy. Laura would be over seventy. His life was more than half over unless he could live until he was ninety-eight. Could he live until then? An old, old man, wetting his trousers and drooling, with his brains a soup.

Once he'd been a school boy. In Boston, the rainy days began in March, and Boston Bay had looked like a mirror that needed resilvering. Walking home in the early dark of the afternoons, his tweed knickers itching so fiercely, his damp socks twisted around his ankles, had he ever thought that life would end? What had he dreamed of when the March rain fell against the windows of the old house on Beacon Street? It was funny that he could recall those awful knickers and the rain and the Bay but not what had been in his mind.

He felt in his pocket for a cigarette. He must be drunk, otherwise the cigarette would be there instead of his daughter's crumpled letter. Laura thought she was the only one who could see through people—he just took longer. He knew damned well that Ellen was already too old for all that nonsense about Paris. She thought she might become a potter, she'd written. He could imagine her, one of those shapeless women in thick skirts who

plunk themselves down on the floor like men, going
all metaphysical and gaga about glazes. It was all so
boring, this creative business, every little plebe with a
sock full of it.

I'm out of it, he thought. I'm going to be old in a year or
two. Why live to be ninety-eight? And girls. He remembered the salesgirl who'd helped him pick out the dresses
for Laura. She'd had a flat rear end, buttocks hanging
down like frying pans. But they'd been *new* frying pans,
and her skin was white as the rind of an orange. Not very
attractive, after all, but young! Not like the beautiful girls,
so perishable, like plums. He was thinking a good deal
about food these days, he noted. He placed his drink on
the table and rubbed his belly. It was growing.

There was a burst of laughter from his wife and her
brother. Their two heads were turned toward him, like
brazen trays on end. He waited for the joke. Then he realized he was the joke.

"Getting fat," he said, and at once regretted the apology
in his voice, hated himself for feeling so thick, so mistaken
somehow, thick with liquor, and it was too late to stop.
They were laughing. He was paralyzed by the sense of an
event re-experienced—standing in front of someone, somewhere, and in the wrong.

"Nothing hurts the fine leather business," he said suddenly. Carlos was already speaking to Peter Rice, but
Laura continued to look at him. The smile was fading,
though. Was she annoyed? Had the silly thing he'd said
about business sounded avaricious? How could she accuse
him of avarice when he hardly knew how the business was
run? The lackeys did it all. And she certainly liked the income, not to mention the fact that he was nearly the sole

support of the mother of these—these colonials. That was what they were, he thought, glaring at Carlos. Colonials, lording it up, maintaining that air of indifference to money and where it came from, until they felt a pinch. Then how they turned! He giggled faintly and turned his back to the room. What a lot of liquor they'd all consumed! *His* liquor. And he'd be paying for dinner too. They'd be laughing and talking in the restaurant, but they'd be keeping a sharp eye on his hands, see to it that he put his hand on his wallet when the waiter came around! He knew all about Laura's greed. He poured himself a shot, leaving an inch of bourbon in the bottle. But her greed was different from anyone else's; everything about her was different. He'd seen her nearly out of her head with desire for some object, then she'd forget it, in a minute, laugh at the extravagance of her own feeling, make fun of herself, take his hand, solemnly report on the general swinishness of the Latin character. She was a great one for that, national character. His own, for example. But she was dead wrong there, all that stupid stuff about the Irish being drunks and liars!

On the night before he'd married Laura, Desmond had sat in the living room of the apartment they'd rented that winter and written down the reasons he was marrying her. At the time, he'd thought it a strange, romantic thing he was doing. He'd even thought of it as a kind of wedding gift, although he'd never let her see it, had burned it in the bathroom a week later. "Middle-class life is boring," he'd written, "and one hardly knows one is alive. My Laura's style—she doesn't count the costs—"

She certainly didn't, not for anyone. Tears came to his eyes; with all her faults, he thought, but a kind of mist settled over his mind. He must pull himself together. His underwear was damp from slovenly urinations, his shirt had lost its crispness (she loved his crispness, she said so often, so unlike Ed Hansen's horrible, perverse frowziness), and he'd nearly lost his appetite. Suddenly, he wanted to drown in alcohol, lap it up, swim in it. He wanted glut!

"Look at that rascal!" cried Laura. He swung around unsteadily. Had she meant him? But she was looking at Carlos. Desmond hated her *charming* voice, the chamber music voice, flute and cello, played for effect, something she only gave a damn for when the stress was becoming a torment. She could go out of control in the blink of his eye. *That* would clear the room! And he laughed again to himself and drained the last of the bourbon.

Peter Rice had been talking about his company, about publishing in general. He would like to have stopped, but there had been some interest, he thought, in Laura, even in Carlos. He didn't want to press anyone with his concerns. He was diffident, and he was already alarmed by some of the things he had said earlier this evening. It was a more nervous occasion than usual tonight. Perhaps it was the girl's presence. It was always best to see Laura alone, a long lunch in the Cuban restaurant he'd discovered that she was so fond of, or a drink or two in the late afternoon in the bar on Third Avenue. He hardly knew what he was saying now, which was what happened when he went on too long, when he knew he was boring. He hardly cared about books anymore. God knows, he had once. Clara had not taken her eyes from him. It crossed his mind that it was easier for her to look at him than at her mother. He smiled at her. Poor girl. Even now, so gravely attentive to the nonsense he was spouting, she gave him the impression of a bewildered spirit, so bewildered she dared not lose track of the dullest conversation lest she miss some clue that would explain her own condition to herself. He knew something about her history, well, he knew the main fact, didn't he? He didn't have to justify Laura—one couldn't judge her by ordinary standards. But he felt sorry for the girl, the unexpected guest who had the door slammed in her face before her eyes could even focus. Hard luck. He'd known both her parents when they were younger than she was now. It was too bad people couldn't know their parents before they were born—they might forgive them more easily. She was smiling at him now, and he realized she had lit a match for the cigarette he was holding. He touched her hand in thanks, thinking, I like her, and instantly, brushed at the lapel of his jacket as though an ash had fallen there. There was no ash; he wanted to rid his fingers of the feel of Clara's skin. He couldn't imagine why he had touched her for a second time tonight, he, who rarely touched anyone anymore, and he was abashed at his glib avowal to himself that he "liked" her. It was simply that he didn't dislike her. Or he had been rattled by the way she'd sprung forward to light his cigarette, had felt the sweat on her hand, known it was from the exertion of trying to please.

Laura was saying he needed a long vacation, and why hadn't he ever gone to Spain? Oh, he would, he would, he promised, tomorrow, next day. Carlos giggled. Peter looked surreptitiously at his hand, the cigarette was half burned down; Clara was back in the chair, gazing at Laura, vaguely smiling. If there was one presence he recognized, Peter thought, it was that of the shabby petitioner lodged inside the accommodating smile, initiator of the lavish gesture. But he might be wrong. The girl had held out the match; she'd been preoccupied with her small task. There was no reason for her to try to please *him*. Perhaps she had a kind nature. And now he was worrying at this trivial incident simply because he'd touched her. Laura was going on about the black corduroy suits the Spanish peasants wore on Sundays; how charming Peter would look with his pale northern coloring in such a suit. There was one who never tried to please people; to net, gaff, and land them— that was something else. Her cheek, when he'd embraced her, had been dry, powdery. It was what he had come to desire, all things dry, ash, dead leaf, stone.

"The bells of Campostella tolling—it is eternity—you must—" Laura's voice idled an instant, rang out in Peter's ears. "You must go to Spain, if only for that extraordinary sound!"

"Probably set off by a button these days," Desmond said aggrievedly. "Probably the button is located in one of those tour buses . . . you know, those tour buses? those terrible women in . . . they wear those big dresses, or those big pants, you know—"

"Desmond, dear. You're straining away there! Isn't he? Poor clouded brains. Darling. Hush."

Desmond clenched his fists. Lowering, defiant, he looked ready to explode. Peter thought, if there's a scene, I'll leave. I'm not up to it, not even for Laura. But when Desmond spoke, he was only fretful, uncertain; it was apparent he wished he'd not said anything at all. "Well—you know—it wouldn't be so strange if they had the bells hooked up to—everything is controlled electronically these days. We've been talking about that. Weren't you, Laura, the end of an era, all that? For God's sake! The bells wouldn't *sound* any different, would they?" And then, importunately, he cried, "Laura? I don't care about the goddamned bells!"

"Good Lord!" Laura exclaimed. "We've put my brother to sleep! Carlos? Pay attention! Look at Clara. Wouldn't she put any woman we know to shame?"

But we don't know any women, Desmond said to himself, Laura's taken care of that. He whinnied suddenly, and stamped his feet, and when they all glanced over at him, he burst into rancorous laughter. "Poor old brute!" he cried. "Stable him in the dark!"

Now he'd frightened the silly girl! He held up his glass so that she could see it. "Empty," he reassured her. "All gone." He'd better sit down a while and clear his thoughts.

Clara watched him struggle with a small desk chair, one of whose legs was caught in a coil of frayed wire that was attached to a standing lamp. He yanked the chair violently. Carlos caught the lamp as it began to topple over, but he did not look at Desmond. No one was looking at him now except Clara. The others were having some new conversation; their voices were extremely loud like people striving to be heard in a noisy crowd. Desmond bowed his head. Clara wondered if he was going to slip from the chair to the floor, to pass out on the rug. He scarcely looked alive, bent in the chair, his face hidden, his thick-fingered hands resting on his thighs. She had never seen him so drunk, so gone, not in all the restaurants and hotel rooms where she had met them over the years. But Laura, apart from a few musical asides about his increasing "muddle-headedness," had not paid Desmond much attention. Perhaps that was what she thought of as "being better" with him. So she had told Clara a year or so earlier in a telephone conversation. Oh—she was getting better, she'd said, wiser than she ever had been with Ed in his cups—learning to leave men alone. "You can't rescue a drunk from drinking," she had said, "you can't rescue anyone from anything."

Clara supposed you couldn't rescue anyone, not in hotel rooms, places that belonged to no one, places of interruption, of immunity from ordinary life where the spirit flags, grows desolate, chilled, but the flesh heats up, flushed, irritated by the odor of license that seems to emanate from *anyone's* bed and bath and pillow, from *everyone's* bastard shelter.

But once she had gone to the rescue, so it had seemed then, to another hotel room, as soft and gray in its furnishings as a dove's wings, where her mother and her father, tense and angry and excited, had waited for her. That had been nineteen years ago. Alma's feet had already become a torment to her. Still, she had taken Clara on the subway from Brooklyn to the bank in downtown Manhattan where they had withdrawn the fifty dollars an old Cuban relative had left Clara in her will. Only two weeks earlier, the two of them had gone to meet the ship which had brought Ed and Laura back from Europe. She had recognized them at once, on a middle deck, leaning on the railing as the ship rubbed its length along the wharf like a large animal.

They had thanked her a dozen times for the money during that half hour in the room over in the hotel in the East Thirties, and she had thought she would go crazy with the excitement of it all; they were as handsome as pirates, the two of them, interrupting each other explaining to Alma about the mistake they had made in choosing the hotel—

but they'd been out of the country for so long—not used to money in the states anymore—and Alma had smiled so much, and rested her feet, and made fun of the little holes she had cut in her shoes so the bunions wouldn't hurt.

Ed got a good job very soon after that, but they never gave Clara back the money. She was glad. It had been a terrible trip to Wall Street with Alma groaning so, moving so slowly. And for some reason, Clara dreaded returning to that bank where the people had been so friendly to her, smiling the way adults did sometimes at children with such intoxicating, if temporary, fondness. She couldn't remember now, if she had told the official there what the money was for.

"A penny for your thoughts," whispered Desmond. He waggled his fingers at her. "Been thinking," he murmured. "You, I mean."

"I'll take fifty dollars," she said, then glanced hastily at Laura.

Desmond guffawed. "That's the way," he said.

"What's the way?" asked Laura, turning toward them.

"Listen—" Carlos interjected. "You do expect that call on time, don't you? I'm afraid it's getting late, late for me. I have an appointment—"

"Carlos! You should have told us earlier," Laura exclaimed. "I had no idea you had someplace else to go. Gosh. We could have made it earlier, couldn't we have, Desmond?" She spoke ceremoniously, rose slowly to her feet, and stood straight, her body still. "And knowing you, you feckless, insulting old bum, we should have ordered up a plump youth to keep you from feeling the faintest pang of boredom—"

"Laura! What a delicious idea! But you're wrong this

time, I'm not bored. Yet. I do have an appointment. Business."

"Business!" Laura repeated incredulously. *"You!"*

"I'm considering opening a sidewalk cafe. I have two chairs, a table—"

They burst into laughter, their large chins pointed toward each other like prows. "And an old toga I could use for a tablecloth—"

"—And the menu," she cried, "nothing but *sopa de ajo*—"

"—*Para todos los vendejos*—"

"—*y los pajaritos*—"

"—*y las putas perdidas*—"

Laura suddenly looked around as if she had just noticed there were other people in the room. "Enough of this spic levity," she said, all formality gone from her voice, her eyes still crinkled with laughter. "Listen, Carlos darling. I must hear from Dan. You know how responsible he is—for five minutes a week. If he makes the call, I'll feel so much easier. If he doesn't, I suppose we'll get a telegram telling us he was forced by circumstances to eat poor Lucy."

Clara laughed, not wanting to, but there was something about her mother's tone—irreverence? Was that it? She had been thinking how adroitly Carlos had avoided a collision with Laura; she had been trying to imagine what it would feel like to be so free with her.

"Eaten poor Lucy," her mother said, no longer smiling.

Desmond heaved a great sigh, then spoke, breaking his long silence. "Oh, for God's sake, Dan will take care of the dog. You know what a fool he is about animals. I mean, why do we have to go on and on about Dan? Who cares about Dan. Stupid . . ." He looked miserable sitting there, hunched up now, staring at Laura, an expression on his face that was both truculent and timid. Laura considered him briefly, then went to the liquor table where she poured out a last drop of bourbon and brought it to him.

"A spring rain," Peter Rice said, looking at the windows. "Or perhaps it's the beginning of the end."

"You haven't said a word about your sisters," Laura remarked. Desmond had taken hold of one of her hands. She withdrew it gently.

"Shall I order more ice?" Desmond asked again, somewhat piteously.

"No, no," she said soothingly.

"Martha is fine," Peter said. "Crazy, though. She went all the way up to Lake Placid just to spend one day with Kitty. New Year's Eve day. To start the New Year together. They're close. I hardly ever see them, even Martha. I think they regard me as an interloper. When Mother was alive— the three women—even when they were girls, they were womanly"—he snickered faintly as though to deprecate any suggestion of a painful reality behind his words—"and when Father and I walked into the living room, they would stop talking, look at us owl-eyed, and laugh."

"That's exotic, isn't it?" Laura asked. "Sister dykes?"

Desmond giggled.

"That's mean, Laura. It's unworthy of you," Peter said.

"Oh no," she said. "No. The sordidness is in your own mind—"

"I didn't say sordid. I said mean—"

"It was the piety in your voice, my dear, faint intimations of complacency—your sisters are so quaint, like those young women who used to fall in love with Keats or Shelley. It is you who are mean. What do you expect if you tell me Martha is crazy? Don't talk fancy, Peter. I've never heard a note of real interest in your voice when you've mentioned those two old girls! I was only going along with the burlesque show."

"One needn't go along with shows," Carlos said.

Laura let out a peal of laughter. "What do you think manners are?" she cried.

"I wasn't putting on a show. Really, I feel quite left out by my sisters. Can't you tell that?"

"Then say so," Laura said with startling coldness. "Don't make me responsible if there's a sting in the responses you elicit. We were *pretending* to speak of your sisters. You needn't have said much. Instead, you offered them up for a giggle or two, and when I giggled, you switched signals."

Clara had trouble breathing—the air was leaking out of the room, draining color from everyone's flesh, faces, and hands and the room furnishings had gone the same ashen color, nothing left to live on but a sweated smoky heat. They were all dying to the vigorous sound of the rain outside. Clara coughed like someone choked with sobs. She could not hear what Laura was saying. Peter was turning his head slowly until he faced Laura. His face looked oddly stretched as though he were holding it in front of him with taut hands. Then he smiled.

"You're right," he said. "Of course, you're right."

"I don't care about that," Laura said.

"I know—"

"I'm so glad you're here. We're such hermits, Desmond and I. How wonderful to see all of you!"

Peter said, touching Laura's arm lightly, "I'm out of cigarettes, I'll go down to the lobby and get some."

"Peter, it's nearly time to go. We can pick them up on the way out," Desmond said.

"No, I want to go down," Peter said. "Really."

Carlos wanted to go too. He needed cigars, he said. He sighed heavily as they left.

The door closed behind them and when the lock clicked, the room was changed as though, Clara thought, they'd been transported to a different place. Desmond swayed to his feet and Clara stood up too.

"Phew!" exclaimed Laura, smiling. "What a relief! Desmond, doesn't Carlos' restlessness drive you crazy? If he isn't depressed, he steams with boredom. Poor Carlos. But in the lobby, he'll refresh himself, ogling at boys . . . not that he'll find much that's classy in a place like this."

"I thought you liked this hotel," Desmond said peevishly. "You never want to stay in any other place except here." He put his empty glass down on a crumpled wet napkin on the table, and when it fell to the rug, he looked at it blankly for a second or two, then made for the bathroom.

Clara picked up the glass and put it carefully back on the table. Her mother looked amused. "Sometimes he makes wee-wee on radiators," she said, then added, "when they're hot. Men and their organs . . . they're endlessly preoccupied with them, aren't they? Unless they're like Peter. Do you like Peter?"

She seemed at ease; she conveyed a promise of some special intimacy, a hint that she would soon say things that would touch upon the heart of one's life, and although Clara knew the promise was empty, that its intention, although authentic, was realized entirely in setting the scene, she was caught like someone who always trips on the same step even as the warning sounds in her memory.

"Yes, I like him. He seems very nice. I hadn't remembered him as being so friendly."

"Friendly!" exclaimed Laura. "He's a eunuch."

"Well, then, a friendly eunuch."

"And Desmond's a drunk," said Laura, lighting a cigarette, "an intolerable, unfriendly drunk. I don't know what
to do. He trembled for a week after the doctor told him
he'd die of cirrhosis, then he took up wine, fancies himself
an expert now . . . I have nothing, no money of my own.
. . ." She sat up, then took her handbag from the bedside
table and opened it. "Look!" she demanded, as she pulled
out and let dangle from her fingers a large Maltese cross
on a chain. "His mother gave me that. I don't know what
it's worth but if he keeps up this drinking, I may have to
hock it. He'll leave me here, you know, without a cent, and
he'll go off somewhere for a week, two weeks."

"But you're sailing tomorrow!"

"We are?" said Laura with such uncertainty in her voice
that Clara, thrown into confusion, rose from her chair and
began to walk about the room. She struggled to find something to say to avert the convulsions of embarrassment
that would afflict her if there was a prolonged silence between them. She found herself standing in front of the radiator; would her stepfather find it attractive? At the
thought, she felt her mouth contort into what she could
only imagine as a hideous smile of malice. But the seizure
passed, and she turned to see her mother staring at the
cross with dreamlike abstraction. Then she gathered it up
by its chain and dropped it into her bag. Once more, she
reclined on her bed, turning her head to look at Clara. If I
let the silence go to its very end, Clara thought, what
would be there? And instantly she flung out a proposal
which she could hardly believe she'd made as soon as the
words were out of her mouth.

"You can stay with me, if he—"

"Oh?" her mother said lightly, with a kind of polite indifference. "Are you still living in that place near Seventieth Street?"

"No, that was just borrowed for a few months. But I thought I'd told you? I have a small apartment on the East Side. I did think I'd told you—"

"You do move about a good deal, don't you?"

The disdain, a hidden charge of rootlessness that she heard in Laura's voice, was a small price to pay for getting out from under her own offer. She resisted with difficulty the impulse to vindicate herself from such charges; she had moved only twice this year, and each time with good reason. And she had a foretaste of that self-disgust, stale, exhausting as a chronic ache, that would arise in her the moment she began to explain—she hadn't had to explain the dress; there, she'd been caught dead out in a lie. For Laura, rationalizations were meat and drink, insults to *her*, feeding a rage which would exhaust itself only when she had demolished the wretched constructions people threw up to conceal what she believed were their true purposes. Ed had said Laura was against reason itself.

"Yes. I do move a lot," said Clara recklessly. Laura made no reply. Defeated, Clara stared at the bathroom door, silently begging Desmond to return.

"He's all right," her mother said grimly. "He's looking at himself in the mirror, thinking about how old he looks." Her voice rose. "I hate the way he pretends! Let him drink, then! Let him rot with it! But the lying . . . and this inertia of mine. I've got to do something . . . something . . ." and she groaned. Clara, hearing that human groan that made her heart beat fast, that she doubted she'd had a right to hear at all, went to the side of the bed. Laura did not look up. Clara sank down beside her, then leaned back until she rested against her mother's body as though some homely intimacy of flesh might calm them both, bring them back into a simulacrum of ordinary life. At that moment, the bathroom door was flung open and Desmond appeared, his face dripping with water. At once, Laura swung away from Clara and sat up, speaking all the while about the phone call from Dan, stretching and smiling and singing her words like an accomplished old adulterer. Adulterer! Clara stood, her head bent down, dazed by that word that had flashed in her consciousness, yet aware, too, of an indefinable culpability. Then, as her mother exclaimed "Why the devil doesn't Danny phone?" the telephone rang and Desmond snatched at it.

"Dan?"

"Darling, I wish I could give you something to drink—or eat," Laura was saying to Clara. "I really should have gotten something, cheese and crackers. I'm afraid we've done in the bar."

And Clara smiled and said, "Oh, I'm fine," wondering what time it was, how much longer before they would leave.

"She fell into the pool?" Desmond cried.

"What?" said Laura. Desmond waved at her, then covered the phone. "I think *he* fell into the pool," he explained. Laura held her head. "Not much of an arrangement," she said. "Poor old Lucy. But, at least, he'll feed her now and then." Then she took the phone from Desmond's hand.

"Danny darling. You've been swimming out of season again . . ." and Laura laughed, her intimate, compassionate I-know-all-about-you, you-darling-born-rascal laugh, that promised comfort and shelter from the others, all the people who knew one only for the debased counterfeiter one was.

From where she was sitting, Clara could hear Dan's shriek, then a high-pitched laugh. She'd met him once, an old Irishman with his sparse hair combed over his forehead. "I live like a tramp," he'd told her once, "but I carry in my mind a perfect room I'll have someday, done in yellow, yellow, yellow like a buttercup, darling, and drapes and flowers, darling, asters and daisies and one touch of eucalyptus green."

Desmond, his gaze falling on Clara, had a sudden thought about her that lit up the drunken haze in his head. He felt suffocated. Oh God! He didn't want to die! Aloud, he said, "Be reasonable! No one's talking about death!"

"What?" exclaimed Laura, turning from the phone.

"Nothing . . ." he mumbled, looking at the empty bottle of bourbon. Laura threw her daughter an imploring look as she said, "Danny, I'll bless you forever, you darling. . . ."

But Clara had heard Desmond. What he'd said was so strange—no one was talking about death—like a riddle, a sentence in which key words were absent, that she forgot for the moment the incident on the bed, the awful sensation she had had of complicity when her mother had moved with such haste at Desmond's return from the bathroom.

The tiny voice from Pennsylvania giggled on; Desmond stared at an empty bottle; Laura looked emptily at the squeaking telephone. Then there was a knock at the door and Desmond went to let the two men in.

Their return altered the polar isolation of the room. It was nothing tangible, only a reminder that in other

regions, other events were taking place. Laura waved gaily
at Carlos and Peter, then began a kind of guttural keen-
ing into the telephone. Jew-baiting, Clara supposed, without Jews, and she recalled how her mother had once said,
upon hearing about a memorial rally for the victims of
Dachau, "How I hate their self-regarding sentimentality!"

"But they *were* murdered," Clara had protested.

Of course, they were all Jewish, Ed Hansen had
claimed, look at your mother's face. Look at it!

And that one time Clara had answered her, she had
looked at Laura's face, which, at her words, had gone cold
and brutish and empty. Then Laura had smiled, and said,
astonishing Clara, "Your suspicion, Clarita, is justified.
The Maldonadas . . . Jews and gypsies, all of us."

Her mother replaced the telephone on its stand.

"There!" she said, and clapped her hands.

"Distraction!" cried Peter. "Food! Cheap entertainment!
Cocktails!"

Carlos rubbed the back of Clara's neck. She patted his
hand, wondering what they were reassuring each other
about, and wondering what it was that always made their
little byplays of affection feel spurious. When the evening
ended, Carlos would go about his affairs. Clara knew he
rarely sought out his sister. Did they ever write to each
other? But she could not imagine Laura writing to someone she could not see standing in front of her.

Desmond felt a touch of sobriety; he breathed deeply; he
sighed with relief. The initial part of this ghastly chore,
this family matter, was nearly completed. The worst was
over. How flushed and pretty Clara looked! She would be
young a long time. The skirt of her dress was like the
petals of a trumpet flower. How beautiful and tense her

long legs were! Then his soul, for a moment so gay, lurched and sank into a dark void. Oh God! Would they never move on, out of this room?

"We decay so," Laura said, looking at her hands. "My fingers look like falcon's claws." She spread them out above the table lamp. "Why can't we age like the other animals do?"

"I think we'd better go," Desmond said.

"At this point, I may not be able to stay for long," Carlos announced with undisguised irritability.

Laura shot him a glance of elaborate amusement, then went into the bathroom and closed the door.

"You do look awfully fine," Desmond said to Clara. "What was it you said you were doing?"

"Won't you come and have lunch with me one day?" Peter Rice suggested.

Carlos said, "Mamá always asks after you. I think she likes you better than any of us. . . ."

Jolted by his words, frightened by the knowledge that they would remain with her long after this evening was over, she looked at him yearningly. Could she explain to him why she did not go to see Alma? Would he help her? Were her self-accusations of inertia just a screen for what was, finally, bad character?

Laura returned, her face freshly made up. She was striking.

"You look wonderful," said Clara fervently, all the long hours, the apprehensions that had preceded this moment forgotten, fallen away. Soon, the door would open.

"Oh, I've always done well with makeup," said Laura, smiling, as she pulled on her gloves, first turning her ring so that it would not catch on the leather.

CHAPTER TWO

Corridor

Desmond checked the doorknob several times, then let his weight rest against the door. Not until he was satisfied that all was secure did he put on his raincoat. The little pause in conversation, during which he'd done exactly as he wished, gave him back a sense of control. Checking locks, straightening his coat, were trivial actions but they were part of a larger preoccupation in him, an animal concern with covering evidence of his passage through his life, a guarded neatness which he abandoned only at the nadir of a long drunken bout. He was brought back to self-consciousness by Laura, who remarked wryly, "Always suspecting crooks." Strengthened, momentarily, by his conviction of having done right, he gave the doorknob another turn. "Hotel robberies are a big business," he said. "Maybe you could get in on it," she suggested instantly.

Carlos, with one gesture of his hand as though blessing his own head, covered his bald spot with his beret. "Shall we go?" he asked with weary patience.

They moved off, Laura walking very slowly so that the others stopped from time to time to mark her progress. Above them in the ceiling was a row of lights, each bulb

embedded in a sentimental plaster rosette giving off a pale
illumination that conveyed an impression of anxiousness.
Clara felt slightly breathless as though the feebleness of
the light was a sign of an ever-diminishing supply of ox-
ygen. She observed slashes in the peach-colored imitation
brocade wallpaper through which had trickled grains of
plaster. Perhaps restless and enraged hotel clients had dug
at the paper with their keys like prisoners who carve messages on the walls of their cells. A harsh red carpet covered the floor. Unlike the other furnishings of the corridor,
it had resisted all signs of human usage. At the foot of a
door they passed a tray holding a dirty plate and a crumpled napkin covered with the blurred orange imprints of a
large mouth. "Whore lipstick," remarked Laura. She
began to whistle stridently. "Christ, darling!" protested
Desmond. Laura kept it up. Then she asked Clara, "Did
you recognize that?"

"Beethoven?" said Clara.

Laura laughed raucously. "Beethoven! My dear, don't
you remember the Paramount News theme? The 'Eyes
and Ears of the World'?"

"She's not our age," Peter Rice said.

Laura gave her daughter a dazzling smile, her face so
close that Clara could see the three plump cushions of her
lips, the large, somewhat dingy teeth, and behind them
the quivering mucosity of her tongue. This intimate view
of the inside of her mother's mouth so bemused her that
she forgot, for the moment, the occasion of Laura's laughter. Then Carlos, taking his sister's arm and pulling her
onward, said he hoped the rain would let up for their sailing tomorrow—so dreary to lumber out of the harbor in a
downpour, and then they all turned the corner. At once, as

though provoked by their presence, a great roaring of voices, a glutinous outpouring of sound flowed out from two open doors and filled the corridor. As they continued on down, they heard a shriek of laughter, stinging and glittering through the confused noise like a thrown stiletto.

"Is that the suite with the wailing wall?" Laura whispered.

"It's a cocktail party, Laura," protested Desmond. "Come on, let's get out of here!"

Three men pushed suddenly into the hall, and at once formed a kind of human teepee from the top of which rose a thin column of smoke.

"We stayed too long in the room," whispered Peter Rice. "Now we have to submit to the ordinary world. Only Laura is rich enough to escape it."

Clara saw a glint of anger in her mother's face. "Rich indeed," Laura said loudly. "Certain seagulls are being beastly this evening and shall not be given their delicious sleepy-time helpers."

Carlos, still gripping Laura's arm, urged her forward, and they walked quickly by the men and the open doors, their faces rigidly averted as though they were passing a pesthouse. As Clara began to follow, one of the three men stepped away from the other two and held up a long, thin cigar in a hand so plump that his pink fingers seemed to have been stuck randomly into the massy fat. "Be careful," Peter whispered to her as he passed. "They'll invite you in."

The man with the cigar was staring at Clara, at the same time brushing the sleeve of his apricot suede jacket. "Aren't you from *Elle?*" he asked. "Haven't I seen you be-

fore? At the party for Michele Trottoir last month? Didn't
I—"

"No," Clara replied coldly. "You've got cigar ashes on
your jacket," she added. The man grinned at her. "Oh,
you're the one," he said. She glanced into a room where, at
the moment, a flock of people fluttered apart revealing a
tall woman who had stretched her arms above her head
and was clicking her fingers. She wore a red dress covered
with sequins. Her black hair was elaborately curled and
lacquered, her eyes sooty like blurred thumbprints, and on
her lips there was an unctuous gleam. She opened her
mouth as if to sing. Several people shouted.

"What's going on in there?" Clara asked the man.

"My God! Don't you know who that is? You're really out
of it."

Clara saw Desmond staring into the second room. An elderly woman wearing a limp black hat rushed out and
grabbed his arm. "Oh, Larry!" she shrieked. "I'm so glad
you came. It's fabulous—she's fantastic—the goddamned
place is full of gate-crashers, but, shit, what's the difference. She's autographed 183 books already. My God!
She's got an arm like a mouth!" Desmond shook his arm
and the woman's hand fell away. "Sonuvabitch!" the
woman cried. "You're not Larry!" He looked back blankly
at Clara, then walked on toward the elevators as the woman retreated back into the room.

"You with him?" the sueded fat man asked Clara.
"Kinda old for you, ain't he? Not that it matters. Right?"
He waved a hand at the room. "In there is Randy Cunny.
Her little life story was published today and we're giving
her a little party. You don't have to be from nothing . . . so

if you wanna meet her? We got all the press here and a whole bunch from publishing and all like you wouldn't believe it." He put an arm around her waist. "Come on, you'll love it!" But Clara pulled away. "Thanks but I'm with some people," she said. She walked on to join Desmond.

"Did you find out what that was about?" he asked her.

"A publisher's party, I guess, for someone named Randy Cunny."

"Randy Cunny!" he exclaimed.

"Is she famous?" Clara asked. At the end of the corridor, she saw that Carlos and Laura were speaking together, their heads bent forward toward each other. Peter Rice was watching them silently.

"She's in the movies," Desmond said with odd reluctance.

"I've never heard of her."

"Sex movies," he muttered.

"The elevator isn't working," Carlos called out resentfully.

"You're so impatient," Laura said with mock severity. "So *American*. It is working. Think! It's that time of evening when people are going out to dinner—the festive time, Carlosito. Listen! I can hear it rattling its cables in there."

"You see? It's gone by again," he said with such misery in his voice he seemed to have forgotten anyone was there except Laura, who would, from habit, allow him a ceremony of disappointment.

"Now, Carlos, a little stoicism, please," she said tolerantly. "Just imagine how would you feel if you were inside a huge airplane brought down in the desert, and no water, and men in burnooses pointing machine guns at you, and you the only Jew among the passengers."

"I'd prefer it to this," Carlos replied sharply. "And I don't have to *imagine* being a Jew!"

Peter Rice laughed suddenly, shortly. At the same time, there was a prolonged screech from the party rooms back up the hall.

"Good God!" Laura cried. "What is going on in there? Are they undressing a coon?"

Desmond Clapper made a shushing sound. "Party," he whispered. "Publisher's party, Peter. You know . . ."

"I don't know," Peter said with such utter disaffection that Clara wondered if she was not hearing the accents of his real mood, a prevailing truth over which he drew a thin cover of amicability, not, she thought, to deceive, but to avoid an indelicate show of some suffering, some estrangement she sensed in him. He was so unlike the Spaniards; everything about him—his different stance, his hands, so clean, so fleshless, so little given to gesture, his plain suit—spoke of a central idea of manners from times past, a strict intention to keep the solitary wounded self where it belonged, in the private dark.

She was aware that Carlos was pressing the elevator button violently, again and again. He turned his back on it suddenly, fell back against it as though it were an insect he could smash with his weight, then stepped forward and raised his hands to his head and clutched his great skull as if he would twist it from his shoulders. Did he keep nothing in reserve except his stupid secrets which everyone knew anyhow?

"What do you mean, you don't know!" Desmond said truculently to Peter.

"Did you get even with the elevator?" Laura asked her brother gently.

"I don't go to publisher's parties," Peter said distinctly but with so pale a human tone, he might have been speaking to a table. "I don't give parties. I have enough between morning and evening of the company of crazed writers shouting out their names on their way to extinction. And if I were the Lord, I would snuff them out in the first sweat of their heat, when their will is aroused—"

"How damned unpleasant!" exclaimed Desmond. "I think I'll go back to that party."

Laura clucked and murmured, "Now . . . now . . ." and drew her coat around herself with burlesque hauteur. Clara saw, for the first time, that it was a handsome fur coat. She recalled, at once, the story of how Laura had gotten it. But she would not think about that now, she told herself. She had suffered enough this night from recollection.

"It's getting too high-toned around here for me," Laura remarked, smiling. "Goodness! All this wonderful male activity! Elevator-baiting, drunken malice, biting the hand that pays one. . . . Really, Peter Rice. How does anyone put up with you? And, see here, no one has told me a word about that party."

"It's for Randy Cunny," Desmond said with dull defiance.

Carlos's bad-tempered scowl gave way to a sardonic smile. "She's the one in that pornographic film, isn't she?" he asked.

"I suppose so," Desmond replied. "A man doll in a suede jacket told Clara she's published a book, an autobiography."

"What a surprising thing you said," Laura remarked. "A man doll! Yes . . . those leathered people. Desmond! How amusing of you."

At that moment there was a loud thud as the elevator doors opened on the floor above them. Carlos was staring at Laura intently. Suddenly, he fell back against the elevator door, his features convulsed with laughter. "Randy Cunny!" he cried as Laura pulled him by the coat away from the door. "Autobiographies! Publishing . . . editors . . . interviews . . . leather . . . the world of literature!"

"What better place for a cocksucker?" asked Laura.

The elevator doors opened. The five silently took their places among a group of middle-aged women in evening dress, each one of whom wore, pinned to her gown, a badge inscribed with her name.

CHAPTER THREE

Restaurant

Carlos and Laura were first out of the elevator. They hurried through the lobby, their arms entwined, grinning, ogling each other, their heads bobbing, fowl-like with laughter, forsaking the others in a fit of mutual appreciation. Behind them, Desmond trailed; reluctance thickened his stride; he looked with contempt at the group of elderly women, who, for an instant, clustered about him, inquiring excitedly of each other the direction of some banquet hall. He could not bear the sweet, dusty odor of talc that wafted toward him from their bosoms and necks. Peter Rice paused at the tobacco and magazine stand and, realizing that Clara was watching him, explained that he always looked to see the new paperback books.

"They're always the same, though the titles change," he said. "Do you need anything? Cigarettes, chewing gum? Band-Aids?"

Her first thought was that Peter was perpetuating the mocking tone of the evening, but then she heard, as though her ears had cleared after an explosion, the obliging plainness of his voice. She thanked him and said no, she didn't need anything. He disconcerted her by patting her shoulder, saying, "It'll go better now. It will be all right in the restaurant."

By now, Clara suspected all that was said to her was equivocal. She had never been able to control the self-betraying part of her nature awakened in her mother's presence, compelling her to submit to a profound intent in Laura to destroy certainty. Clara's ankles felt weak. There seemed no way she would ever get through the revolving doors ahead of her. Somewhere, unimaginably, was the other ordinary life she lived; she grieved for it as though it were lost, stolen. Wearied by division, she was as close to weeping as to laughter.

Peter, who had simply meant to reassure her—she had looked so confused standing there—was alarmed at the naked face of this unknown young woman whose body was inclining toward him so yearningly.

"Shall we move on?" he asked brusquely, and he began to walk toward the revolving doors. Clara followed, vaguely comforted by the touch of damp street air which each revolution of the doors brought into the lobby. She passed an enormous potted fern and, reaching out to touch it, found it to be made of plastic. A bellboy hurried in front of her. Only a few days ago, in another hotel, a bellboy had brought her a message: Room 314. Her silk slip on the arm of a chair, Harry Dana's shirt crumpled on the seat, the outer chill and inner heat of an illicit meeting. She had said, "You wear a ring too?"

"You know I do."

"She gave it to you?"

"It was a double-ring ceremony."

"But who decided on that?"

"Shut up . . ."

"But you loved her, then, didn't you?"

"Love . . ."

"I'm sorry. I shouldn't have brought it up."

"You're angry, not sorry."

"No . . . no . . . I really am . . . sorry."

But Harry Dana had been right. She had been angry.

Peter Rice was saying he wasn't really hungry. "My appetite is simply fading away. I thought I had a fatal disease, but the doctor—" He went through the door, waiting for her just outside. She came through and breathed deeply. Oh, the sweet, rain-washed air! She was dazed with the sense of having been rescued, and she turned, smiling, to Peter.

"—the doctor said nothing was wrong. Age, I suppose. But I remember how nice it was seeing the table set, picking up the fork. . . . How funny! I had my first cooking lesson the day my mother was buried, right after the funeral. I was sixteen, I think, or thereabouts. My father's brother took me off with him to a little stone house where he lived, not far from your mother's mansion—"

"Well!" exclaimed Laura from the sidewalk. A doorman rushed past her to open the door of a taxi which had just drawn to the curb. Laura fell back as though she'd been struck, then she elaborately straightened up. Desmond put his arm around her but she shook him off, her face frozen. Carlos began to walk down the street.

"And," Peter continued, putting his hands in the pockets of his gray coat, "my uncle thought it would distract me to make a pie. Poor fellow, a bachelor, he lived such a silent life there by himself. We decided on a custard pie."

Laura stood unmoving, watching as they walked down the steps toward her.

"It was one of the finest hours of my life," Peter continued. "The old man was so sweet, walking around in
knitted socks my mother had made for him, while we
waited for the pie to cook. I remember exactly how I
felt—I felt that life was hilarious, infinite, glorious! Then
we went to check on the pie—"

"*Will you shut up!*" Laura shouted. An elderly couple
stopped dead in their tracks. A black woman of indeter-
minate age began to laugh loudly, disdainfully, as she
passed Laura. Desmond waved his arms. "Puppy!" he
cried. "Oh, darling puppy . . ."

"Actually, Laura, I wasn't speaking to you," Peter Rice
said expressionlessly. "I was talking to your daughter."
And Clara, who had clutched his arm, felt it tremble.

Laura covered her face with her hands. "I'm sorry," she
said. "I'm so sorry." She looked at the three of them. "It
began to seem we would never get to the restaurant, never
sail on the ship." She smiled, took Peter's hands in her
own. "Oh, Peter! For God's sake, forgive old Laura! Old
fool Laura, Peter?"

He gave her a sign, some gesture of absolution, but he
was unable to smile, only doing something vague with one
hand, a nod of his head, all he could manage against the
antipathy he felt. The savagery with which, a few moments ago in the corridor, she had delivered her "literary"
comment had shocked him because, he had imagined at
first, of her daughter's presence. All evening, he had seen
Clara as an outsider, somewhat pathetic, but young and attractive, and who wasn't a little undone in the bosom of
the family? Especially this family. But wasn't there always
a latent witness in the outsider? And on the face of this uneasy young woman as she had looked at them up there in

the corridor hadn't he seen an expression of utter repug-
nance? Wasn't that why he felt at this moment, after
Laura had behaved toward him with such atrocious rude-
ness, that *he* was the ignominious one?

Self-judgment came over him like a faint into consciousness; he saw himself, an imitator of birds, a middle-aged
man on a strange kind of moral bender that cost him nothing, not even a conventional debasement of the flesh. As
for his protests—prig's squeaks—against Laura's more ob-
vious excesses, her absurd racial obsessions, what were
they but a means of persuading himself of his decency?
His one indulgence, that was how he thought of Laura, in
a life grown bare of delight, narrowed to work and an ex-
iguous care and feeding of his body. . . .

Laura pressed her rain-wet head against his shoulder.
"Darling," she whispered, "you're angry as hell . . ." and
then sighed and asked Desmond meekly which was the
way to the wonderful restaurant?

"Just a block or two south, then west another block," he
replied in an enervated way. They set off. Ahead of them,
down the block, Carlos waited with bowed head. The rain
fell steadily. Empty of the commerce of the day, the sidewalk was nearly deserted; only the traffic went on and on,
a huge dull groan of machinery sounding through the
drone of the downpour. In shop windows things sat on
little spotlit platforms. Among a display of noodles in the
window of a grocery shop, an orange cat stood up and
arched its back. Desmond saw it out of the corner of his
eye; Laura moved against him, large in her fur coat. He
glanced up, above the store. There, silhouetted against a
window, a young woman stood, her hands among the
leaves of a hanging plant.

A rush of memory overcame Desmond, a dark, rich flood

of sensation; a room, his first room away from home, away from college, a couch, a chair, a metal bookcase, his own stove, a table whereon lay an open book, *The Magic Mountain,* a set of keys, his own keys, a pair of wet and muddied boots which he had just yanked off after a walk through Boston Common in the first snowfall of the year, the steamy windows, himself standing in the middle of the room, twenty-two years old, rubbing his hands to bring back the circulation, laughing all by himself, still out of breath from the three flights of stairs up which he had fled taking two great stretching steps at a time. *Now* he knew what he had felt. But then? Had he known he had had the freedom to fly in any direction he wanted? And yet all the strength of that moment, of his youth, had led him to this moment, to the arching cat among the dusty boxes, the girl who was even now retreating like a dream behind the rain streaked windows, to this woman beside him toward whom every motion, every deluded impulse of his life had brought him. There was no way to grasp the reality of the present which slid away each second, invisible as air; reality only existed after the fact, in one's vision of the past. Caught up in the euphoria of his discovery, he turned to Laura to tell her about it all. She was huddled into her coat, her face tight and clenched against the rain. God! How drunk he must be, he realized in that instant, and with all the drunkard's fatuous claim for the singularity of his feelings. He didn't need to talk to Laura about whatever it was he'd been thinking; he needed drinks.

"What about the pie?" Clara asked Peter.

"The pie," he muttered. He looked at her. "But what are you thinking about?" he asked her. "You look so—harrowed."

Disarmed perhaps by such a personal question, she answered him truthfully. "I'm ashamed of myself," she said. "For things I don't do."

He didn't inquire what she meant. He gestured ahead toward Laura who was walking between Carlos and Desmond. "Yes—well, one has to take your mother seriously, but not in the usual sense. It doesn't get one very far, trying to understand her. She is as she seems. But about the pie. I can't think what we put in it, yeast it must have been, because the custard had risen a foot above the crust, like an egg top hat, and when we took it out of the oven and put it on the table, it tipped over—very, very slowly— and bowed to us, touched the oilcloth, and then simply exploded. I can't think when I've laughed so—and my mother just dead."

She had hardly listened. What had he meant? That her mother had to be taken *seriously*? How in God's name did he think she took her? And then he said, "Families hold each other in an iron grip of definition. One must break the grip, somehow."

Desmond paused. "I think we turn right here," he said.

"What do you mean, Desmond, you think?" asked Laura quietly. They had stopped beneath a traffic light on the corner. Laura's chin had a greenish tinge. Then she smiled, forgivingly, it seemed to Clara. It occurred to her that Laura was forgiving them all for being afraid of her.

"Darling, are your feet soaked?" asked Laura. Only Carlos refrained from looking down at his shoes.

"It *is* there," Desmond said. "See?"

They looked down the street where he was pointing. A few yards away they saw a narrow awning and on it the words: *Le Canard Privé.*

"The private duck?" asked Clara.

Laura's laugh rang out. "Be careful how you say that!" she cried.

"It means a decoy," Peter said.

"Wouldn't it be a good clue for a treasure hunt," remarked Laura as she took Desmond's arm. Carlos led the way, a renewed energy in his walk. Soon he'll escape, thought Clara, he's got his great cat's walk back, he's already left us.

Carlos was relieved. His anguished expectation that he would miss an appointment later that evening with a young man from Newark had been a waste of emotion. A minute ago, he'd caught sight of a clock in the window of the dry cleaner's; the evening was not more than a few minutes off schedule, and his patience, though tried, had not yet given way. He would, after all, be able to meet Lance—who had recently changed his name from Leroy as a consequence of a horoscope reading—at the agreed upon hour. Yet he still feared Laura's power to arouse in him a prodigious, engulfing indignation, one that had burst forth in their last meeting some months earlier and sent him cursing from her presence. Blundering into the street, he had run into a pyramid of garbage cans which had left him bruised and covered with rotting things.

"How nice it looks," Peter Rice said, peering through the shadowy window of the restaurant. "Don't you think so?" No one replied.

Inside the restaurant, Desmond Clapper straightened up, looked insolently above the heads of the diners, and spoke a few words to the *maître d';* his tone was cold with the tyranny people display in an environment shaped by their ability to pay. Laura observed him with amusement. They were led to a table, chairs were pulled out, a waiter fussily moved into the exact center of the table a small china duck with somewhat wilted flowers poking out of holes in its back.

Along the walls of the narrow room banquettes were ranged; above them, painted on the walls, were portraits of bewigged young women who gazed down upon the consumers with expressions of faint disdain. Only an occasional clink of plate or tableware troubled the hush imposed by drapery, linen, and carpeting, and among the round tables in the center of the room, dark-jacketed waiters stood poised in the dim light, their pale faces like battered moons.

"Drinks?" asked Desmond importantly, his head raising to summon a waiter.

"Do you know the story of Schopenhauer's porcupines?" Peter asked, smiling. "They were very cold, but when they drew together for warmth, they pricked each other, so they moved away. But they couldn't bear the cold either. So they—"

"I hate aphorisms," Laura said.

"That isn't an aphorism," replied Peter.

"They're all so pompous," Laura continued. "Like this— the impotent man detests the satyr—or—the satyr trembles in the presence of the impotent man—or—between the impotent man and the satyr there is no significant opposition." And she burst into raucous laughter. "You're impossible, Laura," said Peter.

The waiter was bending over them like a beetle inclining earthward from a leaf.

"What'll you have, beautiful kiddo?" Desmond asked of Clara who was sitting next to him. "Well—nothing, really," she said.

"Oh, come on . . . have a bourbon sour. You and me,

that's what we'll have," Desmond said conspiratorially.
"Right?" Peter wanted nothing. Carlos, reluctantly, asked
for whiskey. Laura said they must have a bottle of good
wine. "No stinting, Mr. Clapper," she said archly.

"Don't you want to know what the porcupines did?"
asked Peter.

"I know what they did," Laura said haughtily. "They
compromised on a middle distance. I know how you fancy
such things, Peter, but those silly tales have nothing to do
with human lives. I'll tell you a real story I read in the
newspaper this morning. A man was trying to get into his
apartment through a window. He'd had a fight with his
wife and she'd hidden his key. It so happened he was visit-
ing his lady friend whose apartment was next to his own.
How do you like that! So he climbed through her window,
toward his, and fell four stories to the ground."

"My God! What a stupid story," Carlos said.

Laura spread her fingers out on the tablecloth. "You see,
the trouble was that he'd lost the fingers of his left hand in
an accident. Now tell me a cautionary fable, Peter dear,
about my life, about your life."

"I can't do a thing for you, Laura," Peter replied. But
Carlos looked at his sister with revulsion. "What a morbid
story. I suppose you think there's drama in it. Why, it's
about pure stupidity! You're always trying to put something over, prove the pointlessness of everything . . . was
the man killed?"

Laura, who had been looking at Carlos while he spoke
with an odd intense expression of hope, suddenly threw
her arms around him and kissed his cheek. "Yes, he was
killed," she said as though she pitied not the man but
Carlos himself.

But Carlos wanted none of her pity. He moved back in

his chair, a brooding look of calculation on his face. Laura's story had cast him down, thrown a shadow across his expectations. He had hated both the relentless, triumphant way she had told the story and the story itself—the two females, wife and mistress in separate rooms, the maimed man swinging between them, falling, broken on the street. The future seemed already done with; his anticipation faded. He watched his sister's fingers creeping toward him on the tablecloth. He'd always detested that morbid habit of hers, that staring at and fidgeting with her hands. He felt exhausted! When would Laura give up her pretense that they were a family? One grew out, away from family, the real connections of one's life elsewhere. How sick he was of Desmond's condescension toward him! There was his niece across the table, so milky and moist in her female youthfulness, but her face had the pallor of fear and strain. She was so *humble* with Laura. If he had believed in advice, he would have told her it was the worst way to be. Didn't she sense the power of her youth? But she was still lying there, between her mother's legs, still only just born, weak, helpless. And he thought of his own mother among the old women in the home; they would have been given their supper early like children, and he thought, the enormous voyages of our lives that lead us only back to the beginning.

No one had spoken for a while. Clara shivered slightly, and Peter, on her other side, looked at her questioningly. "Are you cold?" he asked. "No, no . . . it was that ghost that walks over graves. . . ."

Peter unfolded his napkin with fussy care, but he was thinking about something else, hardly aware of what his hands were doing. Carlos saw that the fluttering white cloth had caught the attention of a small, pale young man at the table next to theirs. His head was covered with damp-looking curls, his cheeks and chin were hidden in black facial hair. Slowly, he turned his bespectacled eyes toward Carlos, they were large, expressionless. He was talking to a young woman, talking to her even though he was staring fixedly at Carlos. Carlos leaned to his right to hear what the young man was saying. He was talking about money; the young woman appeared enraptured. Suddenly, the eyes behind the large glasses narrowed and he shot at Carlos a look of dead dislike, at the same time lowering his voice.

Carlos felt cheered. Laura, staring pensively at the china duck, had not seen the little incident. "Peter!" exclaimed Carlos enthusiastically. "Laura mentioned you were going to be made a chieftain at that publishing house of yours? Gosh! Isn't that wonderful?"

Peter looked at him in astonishment. The waiter placed the bourbon sours and the whiskey on the table. "Sure you won't have a drink?" Desmond inquired of Peter.

"I'll wait for the wine," Peter said, still looking at Carlos in surprise. "My old liver . . . Where on earth did Laura get that idea?" he asked. "I'm just an editor, that's all."

"Why don't we have champagne, darling?" Laura asked. "But—gee—I think you might have taken care of ordering wine earlier, you know, when you made our reservation, the way people order birthday cakes." Then, to Desmond's evident distress, Laura began to sing "Happy birthday, dear Desmond," in a deep voice, her face bent toward the table.

"Send the *sommelier!*" Desmond cried to the waiter, attracting the attention of people at several tables. Carlos glanced at the young man. He was clearly making an effort not to look at Carlos. His small, neat hands like the paws of a mouse lay each on either side of his plate. Suddenly he turned, looked straight at Carlos, opened his mouth in a perfect O and bit down, then turned back to his lady friend. Carlos fell back against his chair, convulsed with suppressed laughter. His own childishness made him hilarious. He groaned under his breath.

"I think we're all a bit tight," Laura remarked. "Carlosito, stop trying to pick up that poor boy. Miss Clara, I want to hear more about your job. And as for you, editor Rice—by the way, I never said anything to my brother about promotions—I want to know how the devil you abide going to a job where you detest everyone? Crazed writers, you said. And then Desmond will give you our itinerary, which is marvelous. . . ."

The *sommelier*, a small, frail man, came to their table. He looked as if he had been sleeping in an inclined position and had not yet straightened up.

"I'm feeling a little dizzy," Clara whispered to Peter. "Do you think I should go outside and get some fresh air? It's so close in here."

"Now, don't be cheap," she heard her mother warn Desmond, who was looking at the wine card.

Peter said softly, "It is close but you look fine. Imagine a pond on a spring afternoon, a few trees around it, willow perhaps, a meadow. . . ."

To her surprise, the image of just such a pond slid into her mind, and with it, a bittersweet recall of the outside natural world, the coarse shifting earth upon which squatted these hotel and restaurant strongholds, so close, muffled, airless. Clara breathed deeply and tasted vanilla. She saw the young man at the next table eating a pudding of some sort, taking little scoops with his spoon and after each one, wiping his mouth with guilty haste. He's afraid a bit of dessert will hang from his beard, she thought, with impersonal sympathy—she found his hirsuteness unappetizing—knowing her own fear of mouth-droppings, nose-drippings, eye-leakings.

"Better?" Peter asked. She nodded. "That's awfully good, your pond," she said. "It took me years to find it," he said. "Like the seagull?" she asked. "I invented the seagull in front of your mother's hotel room to amuse her."

Her *mother's* room, her mother's restaurant, her mother's ship . . .

"What will you have to begin?" Desmond asked her with peculiar sentimentality as though she were some dear little thing.

"She wants something with mayonnaise, don't you, Clara?" her mother said.

Peter pinched her arm lightly. She drew away, hearing him say almost inaudibly, ". . . get what you want."

She glanced at the menu. "Hearts of palm," she said loudly.

Slowly, her mother bent her head to stare at the basket of bread; slowly her right hand came out, its heavy, long fingers dropping and closing around a piece.

Clara did not really want anything, but it was a not-wanting full of desperate negative energy. But Peter Rice had been in error with his "get what you want," as if between herself and Laura there was a battle of wills, the older fighting for domination over the younger, mother against daughter. Laura wouldn't have cared if, for an *entrée,* Clara had ordered up a portion of vipers. Clara half

understood—in her head, at least—that this not wanting of
hers was a response, an effort to fend off a huge collapse
that would bring her crashing down against Laura's ultimate indifference. And what she couldn't understand,
what was unplumbed, she felt, but only as a shifting,
bruising weight which so unbalanced her she could barely
trust her voice.

The young man at the next table was drinking coffee
now. A silver link bracelet dangled from his wrist, revealed
each time he took a prissy little sip. Laura was speaking
urgently, as though it were of great consequence to her, of
the collapse of the postal services. But who are her corre-
spondents? wondered Clara. And then of railroad travel.
"You can't get to, simply can't get to, a tenth of the places
you could forty years ago," Laura declared dramatically,
and who would she visit? Clara asked herself. But she experienced only fleetingly a mean triumph in her awareness
of Laura's isolation. After all, it was Laura who chose to
keep herself apart.

Clara ceased to listen. She looked about the restaurant.
The men looked so odd with their inflated haircombs,
vaguely bovine, so dandified. She felt there was something
insipid, hollow in all this *dressing*.

"Everyone wears costumes," she remarked to Peter,
then, with a defensive show of frankness, "Not that I don't
love clothes."

Peter sighed. "Yes. Everyone gets themselves up like
pimps or bums or prostitutes. I don't know what's being
asserted . . . some dim idea about individuality, some
claim that we can be anything we want . . . but then, I'm
timid, and a snob to boot, so I shouldn't—"

"Individuality!" interrupted Desmond. "Christ! They
look alike, talk alike—"

"It's the niggers' revenge," Laura said. "They've taken over the whole country with their clothes and their jail talk—"

"Please, Laura," said Peter, bending toward her. "Don't use that word."

"What word is that?" she asked mildly.

"They're so slow in here," Carlos remarked.

"Now, now, now . . ." Desmond waved his hands doughily. "We're not to misbehave—"

"But you already have misbehaved," Laura said, still gentle, her voice a dying fall of regret.

"Look!" cried Desmond, "here it is! Oh—not for us this time, but it will be along, delicious things . . ." and he fell silent, looking at Laura as though struck with the hopelessness of any appeal.

"Don't say nigger," Peter said insistently. "I hate that word."

"I will have another drink," Desmond vowed.

Laura looked regally at Peter, then past him as though he were not there. "All right, my dear Peter. I know your sensibilities. They're all about *language*, aren't they?"

"I wish they'd bring something," Carlos grumbled. He looked around somewhat wildly, then noticed the young man paying his check with a credit card. He was aware— he knew a great deal about the secret moments of men— that the young man was in an excruciating tension of uncertainty about the tip. His teeth tore at the cuticle of one little finger. The girl was staring up at the wall. "Fifteen percent, dear," Carlos whispered across the few feet of space that divided them.

His sister's hand clutched his. "Oh, don't! Don't . . ." she begged in a low, passionate voice. Her face was only a few inches from his; he saw tears start from her eyes; he felt an answering grief as though they lay wounded together among strangers who could not help them. "I'm sorry," he muttered. And even as she shook her head fiercely, he knew her anguish was not about his teasing the young man, for which he had already condemned himself as senile, cruel, aimlessly self-indulgent. But he drew away from her; his distrust of her was too deep, too habitual, to be shaken off unless, as just now, he was taken by surprise. The unguarded moment between them had been like a flash of lightning which by its very intensity almost obliterates from sight what it illuminates. Whatever he had glimpsed, he was already forgetting it. He wasn't even sure now that he had seen tears in her eyes. She was grinning at him. He felt a worm of self-disgust moving softly in him. The young man and his girl were passing behind his chair on their way out. His behavior had been too gross for an apology. He wondered how long it would be before he had to be kept out of public places. He looked from Peter, to Clara, to Desmond. They were watching the waiter twirl a bottle in a bucket of ice. Someone set a dish of stuffed mussels in front of him. He had forgotten he had ordered them.

"Wait! Wait!" cried Desmond. He held up a glass of champagne. "A toast to Clara!"

Glasses clinked. The moment was lukewarm, awkward. They had all, except for Desmond, been sunk deep in private musing, and the faces now turned to Clara were somewhat vacant. It was harder for her to acknowledge this spiritless amenity than it would have been had their attention been riveted on her. Carlos smiled brilliantly but as though rehearsing for someone not there. Desmond had simply used her as an excuse to get down a drink as fast as he could. He was already reaching for the bottle. The others were merely eating, but Clara felt a sudden conviction that each of them was bemused by an absence; for each of them, someone was missing. It was as if a high wind had dropped abruptly—there was that silence, and everything in a different place. Laura's characteristic expression of always impending irony had given way to a shadowed somberness as she picked in desultory fashion at her dish of shrimp. Clara sensed in Peter a subtle, tenuous curiosity reaching toward herself, but from Carlos, nothing, no further interest, their ritual recognition performed hours ago in the hotel room.

Anxiously, she touched Peter's arm. "I was interested in what you were saying—about clothes . . . do you really think people feel they can be something else, different, just because of what they're wearing? And what is it they think they are to begin with? And what do they want to be?"

"It's the absence of thought that makes this costume dressing so vulgar," he said. "These masquerades—nothing but celebrations of the masks themselves, no idea—it becomes a matter of who has the most feathers."

"Then there's your plain blue suit," remarked Laura. "Just snatched it off the rack, did you, Peter? Really! I'll bet you ten dollars it took you a year to find a suit like that. What are *you* celebrating?"

"Listen, I'm sorry to press, but we haven't ordered yet. I have an appointment—" Carlos began.

Laura snorted. "A what?"

"—and I'd rather not be late," he went on imperturbably.

"And we must have more wine," Desmond said quickly.

He waved his hands in the air, averting his eyes from Laura. Several waiters converged upon their table. Desmond laughed benignly. "More of this!" he cried to the waiters, flapping his fingers toward the empty champagne bottle. "More of your special marked-up wonderfully overpriced blank de blank—right? Now ladies and gentlemen, what about—"

"I would like the trout," said Laura to Desmond, but the others spoke directly to the waiters who repeated their orders to each other with gravity and precision. "That chicken is really ready, isn't it?" asked Carlos. "I'm in something of a hurry—"

"Everything was cooked a week ago," interrupted Laura, "in order to allow the waiters to go on strike should they wish—"

"Scallops?" Clara said to one of the waiters.

"Perfect," he said. *"Parfait,"* murmured the other. Laura laughed softly.

"Well, Peter . . . let's get on with it," Desmond demanded. "Where's our wine?"

"Veal chops," said Peter.

"And I . . ." said Desmond, and fell silent. Laura gave him a look of mock wonder. "Oh, tell us, dear man! What?"

"A duck," said Desmond, his eyes on the wine now being opened by a waiter. "No. Not a duck, but *filet mignon.*" He looked over at Peter. "How boring of you, really. Veal chops! For God's sake!"

"You may order for me," Peter said amiably.

But Desmond was drinking champagne, his eyes closed.

"There's a farmer who lives near us," Laura remarked after their glasses had been filled. "He wears brassieres under his work clothes. Now, what would you say was his idea, Peter?"

"I wasn't talking about that kind of aberration," Peter said.

Laura laughed scornfully. "Oh, you weren't, were you? That kind of aberration, is it? Tell me about· your plain, restrained, fastidious blue suit! You are a self-righteous, sententious bastard, aren't you?"

Clara found herself smiling uncontrollably. Laura was awful! *Awful.* Yet Clara couldn't stop smiling.

"The incidence of torture is rising all over the world. Did you know that, Laura? I'm beginning to suspect you're behind it," Peter said.

"Something to do with the dignity of man, isn't it?" Laura asked pleasantly. "But your suit—"

"I would like to stop talking about my suit," Peter said flatly. "It's ten years old. It's something to keep the rain off of me. As for my self-righteousness—it's harder on me than it is on you, and if you like, I'll take myself and my suit and leave."

"Oh, Peter!" she cried, holding out a hand toward him. "Oh, I was only teasing. God! You *know* how glad I am you're here! You know how *foolish* I am! Desmond! Will you *stop* throwing down that champagne? Peter, listen!" But she fell silent, her hand still held out, palm up, her eyes pleading. Peter reached out and touched her fingers with his own.

"It's all right," he said.

"Is it all right?" she asked wistfully.

He nodded. He'd known how she'd react to his threat to leave. It had been safe, a signal to her that she'd pushed him far enough. Sometimes she flew at him like that, but almost always about qualities he detested in himself. He was safer with Laura, he often told himself, than with people less suspicious of themselves than he was. Of course, there were some things she couldn't do; he would not go along with *nigger;* he would not sanction the brute in her. But they understood each other; she was ruled by impulse, he, by constraint. And each pitied the other for their subjugation to opposing tyrannies. And this opposition between them—wasn't it the reason for the durability of their connection? Their undiminished interest in each other?

Clara, against whose thigh Desmond had, perhaps accidentally, pressed his own, moved closer to Peter. He heard her breathing, caught a whiff of some mild floral scent she was wearing, and realized that his hands were clenched.

"You haven't told them about the letter," Laura said to Desmond.

"You've told them enough," replied Desmond sulkily, his eyes on his empty glass.

"You should read it to them, darling. The former Madame Clapper's daughter is so *like* her. The style is different, but not the temperament. God, Clara! I hope you're not like me!"

"We all hope that, Laurita," Carlos said playfully. She seemed not to have heard him. In any event, the waiter had just arrived with their orders, and Desmond was busy and important, ordering another bottle and announcing who had ordered what.

"It doesn't look good," he said. "I can tell it's not hot, either."

"It's perfectly okay," Laura said breezily. "But this fish looks a bit morbid, doesn't it? Look how they've poked a bit of parsley through its eye. Well—about the letter—"

Desmond dropped his fork and bent heavily to find it.

"Don't pick it up from the floor," Laura said brusquely.

He looked at her with bleary uncertainty. "In my lap," he muttered. His lower lip was hanging slightly open. Then the waiter came with another bottle of champagne, and Desmond smiled childishly. It wasn't fair to judge him when he was so drunk, Peter told himself. But he couldn't help being struck by how little variation there was in Desmond's facial expressions. He was like some toy you could bend or wiggle, a little mannikin with blank painted features. He saw Laura glance at each one of them, then at himself, as though she were calculating their substance. He wished she'd drop the subject of Desmond's daughter. What was she trying to make Desmond admit?

"She flatters poor old Desmond so, or tries to—all about the people he must have known in Paris. . . ." She smiled companionably at Peter. Then in a falsetto voice, she cried, "Oh, Da! Tell us! And did you meet the great G. Stein?"

"Please stop, puppy," entreated Desmond.

Laura scowled at her plate. Then she glanced at him mildly. "Oh, the devil with it," she said.

Peter noticed that Clara was not eating; her hand rested near his plate. "Aren't you hungry either?" he asked.

"Not very," she said in a tired voice. She couldn't very well explain to him how frightened she had been that Laura would go on and on about that unknown daughter, how strangely implicated she felt by Laura's attack on that girl.

"We're all beggars, pinching each other," Peter said to her in a whisper. She looked at him in surprise. Had he meant Laura? She said, "I was just thinking—"

"You were, were you?" her mother asked archly. "And what thoughts were those?"

"Dinner thoughts," Clara said quickly.

"I don't think she is like me," Laura said thoughtfully. "Do you think so, Carlos?"

"Not in the least," Carlos replied decisively.

"Yet it's hard to escape . . . you think you're different, and you end up, fatally, so like them," Laura said in a removed, dreamy voice. "When I was in the hospital years ago, Mamá came to see me." She began to eat, not looking at anyone. Was that all? Clara wondered. For a while, no one spoke.

Carlos had eaten all the chicken he was going to eat. Soon, he estimated, he would be able to order coffee and make his getaway. There was no reason for Laura to make a scene at this point. He'd put in his time. And actually, when he thought of it, she wasn't much given to scenes anymore. Her temperament had cooled, softened. And that astonishing discernment she had—the way she could sense in him a thought, a mood, gathering up in one intuitive flash the whole sum of his feeling—once the servant of her vindictiveness, had been tamed into an irony not inconsonant with his own.

Sometimes, late in the evening, she telephoned from Pennsylvania, and they often spoke at length, and companionably. He was often fond of her. He began to smile, recalling an incident from those old bandit days of hers. Then, he had thought it extravagantly comic, and told it to anyone who bothered to ask him what his sister was like. It must have been over a dozen years ago. Laura had found out Desmond was involved with some woman. She'd confronted him. He'd denied everything. She'd begun by breaking every dish in the apartment they'd been living in, smashing and tearing and ripping—"I razed the

wretched place," she told Carlos later. How well he'd
known that depth of loathing, of violence in her. Even
when they were children, he'd hidden from those great
drowned eyes of hers and covered his ears to shut out the
terrifying things she could say. Desmond had finally fled
the apartment. She had torn her own dress into shreds;
she had already destroyed whatever she could lift and
throw. Then she'd gone through Desmond's jackets and
found his address book where he kept the names of
various clients in stores all over the country. All the good
shops carried a few pieces of the luxurious Clapper
luggage. She'd had some money that Clapper had given
her earlier to buy liquor the next day. She'd gone to a
Western Union office. "You know how vain poor Desmond
is," she said to Carlos. "He's *furtive,* too, you know. And
the *Shadow* struck!" She had sent thirty telegrams—not
enough money for all the names in the address book, she'd
explained regretfully. The message had been identical: *Am
in desperate trouble. Please send $2.00,* and signed it, *Des-
mond Clapper.*

"The Shadow . . ." he uttered with a certain rueful affection. Laura looked at him blankly. He began to fold his
napkin.

"What are you doing, Carlos?" she asked. "You don't
have to tidy up. Desmond is going to treat us all!"

"Actually, I'm going to have to leave soon," he replied
pleasantly, socially.

"You'll have some brandy with us," Clapper urged.
"Here, wait—"

"But Peter and Clara are still eating," Laura said reprov-
ingly.

"Shortly," said Carlos. "I didn't mean this instant."

"I started to say something, didn't I, Desmond? About Mamá? When I had the operation . . ." Laura placed her cutlery in the middle of the plate. "My memory . . . but, oh, I remember now. The day after the operation, that miserable second day, Mamá came to see me. I was nearly senseless with pain, and in that drug daze, you know. And she said, 'In Cuba, there is an herb. . . .' *In Cuba*. And there I was, groaning on a hospital bed in New York."

"Yes," Carlos said. "I see what you mean."

"I should think you would," his sister said in a low bitter voice.

"'Toma leche,' that's what she always told me," Clara said eagerly, sensing a chance of some community of feeling. "Even after I gew up, when I'd go to visit her in Brooklyn, one time when I fractured my wrist, she looked at the cast and she said, 'Drink milk,' yes, that's what she always said."

"The *futility* of it," Laura began. Then she grew silent, staring across the table at Clara who moved back into her chair, her eyes widening as though something had sprung at her and halted in mid-air.

Her voice metallic, serrated, Laura asked, "And did you? Did you drink milk?"

Desmond, half drowning, half swimming in the new wave of drunkenness brought on by his cunning appropriation of most of the champagne, was still sentient enough to feel a sudden, dangerous tension. He emerged from the liquid depths of his mind like a deep-sea diver bursting through the surface of the sea. "Eugenio!" he cried, offering this pearl to Laura. "He lives behind his office, did you know, Peter? Like one of those candy store fellows . . . and tells himself stories of the Maldonadas, how they fell

out of the Pyrenees like *cucarachas.*" He laughed extravagantly—it had been the right move, they were all smiling
at him—and gratified, he repeated, *"Cucarachas . . ."*

"Did you ever hear such an atrocious accent?" said
Laura, "and just look how pleased he is with himself!" She
patted his hand. He pulled it away, offended, but he was
mystified by his sense of injury, and that made him angry
too. Let them have at each other, he said to himself, I
wash my hands of the lot.

"Has my sister mentioned de Rojas to you, Peter?"
Carlos asked, grinning. "The other branch from Cadiz.
Consider our noses, hers and mine. *Nariz de Cadiz.* And if
today was Friday, well, then, some cousins of ours in
Cadiz would light the Friday candles behind closed shut-
ters—"

Laura interrupted him with a mirthless laugh. "My
brother has a perverted sense of romance—among his
other perversions," she said. Carlos laughed as though
Laura had paid him a compliment.

Clara observed the waiter looking at their plates. She'd
left most of the scallops; they had been prettily arranged,
but cool, overseasoned. At the front of the restaurant, the
maître d' bent over his list of reservations. A group of people suddenly entered, and his head rose up like an animal's rising in high grass.

"She fancies herself an Arab," Carlos said. "Laurita, you
know the Arabs are Semites, darling, don't you?" He
couldn't think why he was trying to provoke her, now that
escape was so near. And he was nettled by her clear-eyed
smile, by the caressing little chuckle she gave.

"Those poor Arabs," said Desmond mournfully, thickly.
"Nobody cares about *those* people—"

"That reminds me," Laura said. "I saw a group of—" she paused and smiled at Peter, "—of *Negroes* marching along the street this morning. They were all wearing fezzes! Imagine! They seem to have a fatal attraction toward the world's champion slavers, don't they? Isn't it comic? And they looked so self-important, shuffling along in their Arab getups. What a joke history is! I wonder where they were going."

"And all these Jews," Desmond said insistently, "living here and sending money there. What right have they got—"

"Desmond, you don't know anything about it," Laura said as though amused. "Why shouldn't *they* be there? History is nothing but thieving and slaughter. Why shouldn't the Jews have a go at it?"

"Laura," he protested, "I do know—I—"

"Here's our waiter," said Laura calmly. "Clara, have some rich dessert."

"No, thank you. I'm really full—it was delicious—but, I'll just have coffee."

"Hush," said Laura cryptically.

"Coffee," said Peter to Desmond who was clutching a menu. How grotesque Laura was, reversing herself like that, not that he wasn't used to it. Her inconsistency was constant. But Desmond was something else. Peter realized how much he really disliked him, his bog anti-Semitism, that special kind of Irish bog-hatred, stinking of rank weed, eyes glittering with the conviction there were creatures even lower than himself.

"We'll all have brandy, won't we?" Desmond was saying, failing to hide his eagerness. "I hope you noticed that I've not been smoking, Laura," he added.

"Then you forgot your cigarettes," she said.

"Bring me some damned cigarettes," Desmond said resentfully to the waiter.

"What sort, sir?"

"Anything."

"It should be *what kind*, shouldn't it?" murmured Laura to Carlos. He was lighting a cigar. He reached over and dropped the small paper band next to Clara's champagne glass. He'd always done that, given her those little paper rings from his cigar. But her hands had grown too big now. She felt regret, but for what? The small hands of a child? For the lost illusion that Carlos was giving her something of value?

"The torte is excellent tonight," the waiter said. But he was not looking at any of them, he was staring bleakly at the doors through which a large crowd of people had just now arrived. They were making a good deal of noise. The *maître d'* did not even look up from the table where he kept his list of reservations, and Clara felt alarmed at his neglect of these new arrivals, almost as if they might blame her.

"Or the mousse," the waiter said, barely restraining his impatience to be off. Laura looked up at him and smiled, waiting until she'd caught his attention.

"Are you in a hurry?" she inquired politely. "Do you want us to leave because all those ladies and gentlemen have come? Goodness! This must be a very famous restaurant!"

"Of course you don't have to leave," the waiter avowed in a low, urgent voice. Alarm had yanked him out of his waiter's remoteness; he was suddenly *too* present; even his breathing was audible.

"And it is what *kind* of cigarettes," Laura informed him evenly.

"I'll have coffee, please," Peter said quickly.

"We'll all have coffee," Laura said, "if you can spare the time."

"And brandy," Desmond said. "You'll have brandy, won't you?"

No one answered him. "A good brandy," he muttered. But the waiter had gone.

"I wasn't going to have him fired, Peter," Laura said.

"Your quibbling frightened him," Peter replied.

"I wasn't quibbling."

"You were bullying him," Carlos said. "You were behaving like a peasant."

Laura looked worried, humbled. "Carlos, no! It wasn't bullying. But he was trying to rush us away! Did I really behave badly?"

She actually can't judge her own behavior, Peter thought; she explodes, then wonders at the flying glass. But he didn't believe anyone but Carlos could have spoken so severely to her, because the rest of us, even Clara, are foreigners, he thought, but Carlos, though she could be savage with him, could sway her merely because he was her brother, his presence invoking their common origin, that intense accidental intimacy like no other, the cruel affinity of family. He felt worn, frail; beneath the evening's surface, something hidden was draining him of the capacity to respond. He had always counted on Laura to rescue him, for a little while, from shallow custom, to revive in him a memory of the life of feeling, but this night, the constantly erupting flares of a temperament he'd always thought to be without calculation or prudence seemed merely a mechanical display.

"Hines. I'll get Hines brandy," Desmond said. Then, an offended host, "I don't understand you people. Do you or don't you want—"

"Get it! Get it for yourself, for God's sake!" Laura hissed at him.

Clara tore the cigar band she'd been fiddling with. There was a taste of butter in the air, and of meat. Desmond's hand closed around her arm. "Hines brandy," he whispered. "Good stuff!" She could think of nothing to say. Eventually, his warm, suety hand fell away.

"But we were talking about my brother Eugenio," said Laura loudly.

"I wasn't," Carlos said, laughing. "I never talk about Eugenio if I can help it."

"But you've seen him?" Laura asked.

Carlos looked guarded. "Well—yes. I don't remember quite when—"

"I have a reason—"

"He'd bought himself a suit. Awful! Like an undertaker's suit. He came to see me, as a matter of fact. I heard him tripping over the stairs. You know how he always trips on every third step?"

"Because Desmond is being driven mad trying to get hold of him. Do you know we had to send him a telegram last month about his share of Mamá's expenses? His own mother! Why should poor Desmond be left holding the bag?"

"He takes frequent trips," offered Carlos lamely.

"On every third step?" Laura asked with grim humor.

"Look," Carlos began, "this isn't a subject for general discussion—"

"General discussion," cried Laura. "Peter. Excuse me. But this is unendurable. You don't know how we have to *beg* those two to help their own mother! Clara, Clara! Do you know how she *asks* after you? How uncomplaining she is? How little she expects? Oh, how *right* she is to expect nothing . . . nothing. If it wasn't for Desmond—"

"Stop it, Laura. Stop it! In fact, I'm going to visit her tomorrow—" Carlos protested.

"Tomorrow!" cried Laura, and her eyes rolled up, her mouth gaped, her hands went to her face where they pinched and kneaded her flesh as though to force it to the very bones. Desmond, snatched from his drunken reverie by his wife's frenzy, shot enraged looks at the others—who was to blame for setting her off this time?

The waiter arrived with coffee which he served them with anxious solicitude. Then he held up a piece of dark cake and looked questioningly at each of them. No one had ordered it, but Peter claimed it hastily. Laura had let go of her face and sat, as still as death, staring down at the tablecloth.

"I was forced to go and plead with the welfare people," she began in an expressionless voice as soon as the waiter had left them. "My mother's sons are shiftless men—too tight to have gotten married. Imagine becoming a homosexual to avoid supporting a woman!"

Carlos's expression of patience in defeat didn't change. In a certain way, he seemed to have deafened himself to Laura's words, although bearing the anger that shaped them as a familiar and ineluctable discomfort. He murmured something to her that no one else heard. A silence that contained a faint suggestion of a truce descended over them. Clara grew aware, with an easing of her spirit, that there were other people not much more than an arm's length away, small islands of people at their tables, among whom waiters eddied and shifted, bent and straightened up. Some of the diners looked domestic, some festive, and some were silent. How, she wondered, did this table appear to all those others? In the subdued ambiguity of the restaurant lighting, the sustained clamor of conversation and eating, would anyone glancing casually at the Clapper table have observed the ravages of the battles that had raged among them? And was the apparent placidity and self-satisfaction of all those other people only a contrived show?

Clara had been frightened, but Laura's reproach to her had been contained in the larger attack on Carlos. For the first time, she suspected that Laura had no real expectation she would visit her grandmother, but there was no consolation in the thought, no sense of freedom, only a feeling of being adrift.

By then, Desmond had finally managed to order brandy all around. Carlos and Laura were speaking somewhat listlessly about a movie they had both seen, quarreling a little but without interest.

"Do you have an extra cigarette?" Clara asked Peter. He pushed his uneaten piece of cake aside and handed her a pack, then took it back and opened it for her. She took the cigarette somewhat rudely, sticking it into a corner of her mouth, lighting it at once before he had a chance to. She looked at him slyly.

"Sorry," she said. "It's disgusting, isn't it? This getting the thing into the mouth?"

"How long have you worked for your agency?"

"Half a year," she said.

"You don't care for it?"

"No. I don't see how one could be devoted to such work. It's all deception, really. It's not like publishing books. I imagine you must get something in you really like once in a while, don't you?"

"Once in a while," he replied. He watched her take a sip of brandy. She suddenly reminded him of someone—but, of course! She had Ed Hansen's nose! How odd he hadn't seen it before! Even odder that he hardly ever thought of Ed Hansen anymore. It must be over fifteen years since he'd seen him, and then, only briefly. It was not a period of his life he liked to reflect upon. He had just been separated from his wife, had just begun working for the publishing company, and had just abandoned a novel he had nearly finished. In the room he had rented after he'd left Barbara, there had been a small, cheap, heavily shellacked desk. Day by day, the pages of his story had mounted up. Then, when he'd come to the last chapter, terror overtook him. It was as though the pages had occupied a space in his body now left empty by their appearance on the desk, an emptiness into which he collapsed. He'd almost gone back to Barbara. Instead, he'd looked up the Hansens, who were in the city temporarily, and discovered them in an acrimonious, racking argument about whether to go to South Carolina or Long Island. They hadn't been of much use to him then. And within a year or so of that night, they had been divorced. Hadn't it been more like twenty years ago? For too long he had relinquished his own history; now he couldn't separate out the years, the events. At best, his connections with other people were frayed; except for this long friendship with Laura, his life felt nearly motionless.

"Laura," he said in sudden agitation, trying to push away the haunting feeling of time lost, times forgotten.

"I'm here, darling," she replied at once, smiling at him with an extraordinary tenderness as though she sensed, and wished to assuage, his distress. But *was* it his distress which had elicited from her the thrillingly spoken endearment? He was not comforted, he was alarmed. Was it not that he had revealed, for an instant, a true state of feeling, had abandoned the posture of being her temperate adversary? And if it was that she had recognized, what difference did it make whether she called him *bastard* or *darling*?

"Well! Are we ever going to hear about this trip?" he asked aloofly. It didn't work; he felt the weak core of his own voice, and so did she. Her gaze was knowing, amused.

"Why, yes," she said. "If you'd like to hear about it. . . ."

The radiant names of ancient cities blazed up among prosaic details of hotel and travel arrangements. Laura, with a peculiar, uncharacteristic thoroughness, seemed intent on giving them an odyssey of timetables.

Clara drank her coffee and smoked Peter's cigarettes. The waiter returned to fill their cups as they were emptied, and when he was not occupied with his other tables he stood close by, glancing covertly at Laura.

Out of the conversation between Peter and Laura which neither involved nor implicated her, safe from any foggy overtures from Desmond—who sat beside her, half asleep, a feeble intermittent smile widening his mouth from time to time—she resolved to think about Harry Dana. She summoned him. He would not come. Silently, she recited certain features of her lover's body, the tight white skin across his cheekbones, his nipples like bits of coral, a small, livid scar on the arch of his right foot, his large, clean, rather characterless hands. But these talismans evoked nothing of Harry. Instead, and unbidden, a figure came slowly down a long corridor toward the light of her recognition. It was her grandmother, one hand gripping the handrail which ran through all the halls of the old people's home, an aid to aged infirmity, an iron insistence upon it. Clara glanced across the table at Laura. "By train, then we take a special bus . . ." she was saying.

The passionate accusations Laura had made against her brothers for their neglect of Alma might never have been uttered. Yet, by what right had she made such accusations? For years, she had been away; it had been as though she were dead. What could she have known of that street where Clara and Alma had lived? Stores closing one after another because of the robberies, the only market eight blocks away, the cars that didn't stop for traffic lights as though it were a territory accursed, the piercing stench of abandoned cats who often sheltered in the foyer, the entrance doors always ajar, even in the cold weather, and in the summer, letting in a limp breeze charred by the exhaust of cars, carrying a faint, stale damp, smelling of wet ashes. People moved out; the heat was failing, the electricity intermittent, misshapen castaways turned up, announced themselves as the new janitor, then they too disappeared. But there were others; the wood panels of the elevator grew ever more scored with their proclamations—threats, sexual offers, names, numbers. Yet in the last year Clara had lived there, Eugenio was the only person she had ever seen in the long, narrow tiled halls. He always carried a briefcase; he would bow to her and step hastily away.

On Sundays, Carlos and Eugenio would come to a midday dinner, although if Eugenio was living in the apartment, he would leave early while Alma was still cooking. And often, when he did stay, he would leave abruptly at the meal's end, giving a stiff salutation to each of them as he placed a small hat on his head.

They ate in the dinette, a space only large enough to accommodate a small round table and four straight chairs. There was a window there, but a thickly rusted fire escape deflected most of the light. The cooking area was a narrow passage between wooden cabinets stacked up like crates. The top ones had never been used, not even opened. Here, Alma moved arthritically, sometimes singing to herself, sometimes so wounded in her hopes that her crippled hands lost what strength they had to lift pots and set them down.

In the airless, tight space of the dinette, her two sons sat upright like prisoners about to be interrogated. They rarely spoke. Clara spent as much time in the tiny kitchen as she could to escape the dreadful tension at the table, the grim look of the two aging sons bent over their meal while Alma chattered of neighbors no one had ever seen, stories in pictorial magazines no one cared about, odd bits of information from radio programs no one wanted to know. Perhaps it hadn't been simply tension which had driven Clara into the kitchen, perhaps it was the unbearable suspense, the torment of each Sunday, of whether Alma would, at last, get and hold their attention, win a reprieve from her recognition that they were merely submitting to her, that their filial piety did not dissipate an outrage that utterly baffled her. So she would redouble her efforts to please them, at the same time allowing the strain of those efforts to show, a reproach to their hardness of heart which, in turn, only grew harder. Sons and mother, a jigsaw of misery fitting together perfectly. Yet she required their presence, enforced it in a dozen indirect ways, battling against them with her smiles, her jokes, her helplessness. She knew of Carlos's grave but somewhat ironic interest in monkeys. She cut out photographs of apes and gave them to him with flirtatious smiles.

Alma did not know—as far as Clara knew—that Carlos had once been arrested while, he had claimed, he was watching the antics of the monkeys in the Central Park Zoo. But a huge, fat youth had sworn that Carlos "fooled with my behind." The charges were dropped; the youth, Ed Hansen had told Clara, had behaved repugnantly in court, the judge had dismissed the case. Actually, all the Maldonadas were diverted by monkeys which, after all, reflected a human ludicrousness in their simian antics. Why wouldn't they appeal to people who held up even their own behavior as sardonic evidence of the profound silliness of humankind?

Once in a great while, Carlos would bring along a young man friend to a Sunday dinner. *"Pero que sympatico!"* Alma would whisper to Clara as the young man handed the old woman a bouquet of flowers smelling faintly of subway kiosks, or little boxes of glacéd fruit; later, the young man would hold her hand and tease her gently about her accent.

And sometimes Eugenio would break the granite monot-
ony of the meal with a report from the world, a dinner
party he had attended. Always, the silver was old, invalu-
able, worth a fortune. "A fortune!" he would repeat again
and again, staring down at the rice and black beans on his
plate, or at the thick, plebeian water tumbler, or at the
mean cutlery. After they left, Alma would retire to the bedroom and undo the ties of her black shoes and lie down,
staring up at the ceiling, and Clara, drawn there despite
her reluctance by the old woman's plaintive sighs, a fitful
breeze of sorrow, the only sound that broke the silence of
those late Sunday afternoons, would stand in the doorway
repulsed, dismayed by the long white strands of hair
which had worked themselves loose from Alma's hairpins
and fallen about her cheeks and neck.

What could Laura know of those Sundays, of the slow,
soft dolor of Alma's forlornness, of the daily life of those
two rooms from which, each Monday morning, Clara made
her escape to the public school classrooms? How dared
Laura claim exclusive right to pity Alma now?

"It's bad luck you weren't born grown up," Ed had once
remarked to Clara. "Your mother detests natural helplessness." When Ed was ill, he said, Laura often disappeared
for days at a time. He seemed amused by that, as though it
were merely idiosyncratic. Clara chose not to inquire what
he'd really felt. And Clara had learned that it was not only
"natural helplessness" that Laura hated. Her dread of any
kind of insufficiency in the world was so intense that even
what she judged to be bad taste could put her off someone,
as though weakness of aesthetic judgment or simple ignorance in another person, placed *her* in mortal danger. But

of what? She had taken care of old Mrs. Clapper, but even in her dissolution, the old woman sounded tigerish, and after all, there'd been an advantage in it.

"Clara?" Carlos was bending over. "Goodbye, darling," he said. "I'm leaving you to your mamá." He was smiling. He looked happy.

"Carlos," Clara said pleadingly, "do you have to go?"

"Come and see me soon," he said, turning from her, moving off toward the doors. No one, she thought, was ever more lighthearted at the moment of departure than Carlos. She felt chilled. Their party had been drastically altered, more, it seemed, than could be accounted for by one empty place at the table. Affectionate, secretive, swinish Carlos! It was always easy to miss him; he left behind him no bitter echoes.

Laura was rolling a bit of bread between her fingers. Peter tapped his brandy glass with one finger. The tiny clang was like the distant sound of a buoy. Laura began to speak to Desmond in a low voice, her words inaudible. Soon, Clara would leave. By the time she unlocked her own door, the evening would begin to be unreal—or unrealizable. She would, when she thought of it, remember what she always remembered, her uneasiness, Laura's old thunder, and a sense of self-betrayal that would linger on a few days, a week, until it was buried away, yet persisting on in dreams of mortification or in moments when she could not look directly into someone's face. She had tried to describe her mother to Harry Dana. She had not thought Laura would seem boring to him. He said he didn't like the way her voice sounded when she talked of Laura. What did he mean, she had asked. He had said he didn't know quite what he meant—portentous or elaborate, something like that. Thinking about that now, she felt irritated, restive, unjustly charged. She had only been trying to divert him.

Yesterday, Harry had stopped by in the early evening. They had embraced poignantly, as though in a great reconciliation. Their hands, as they fondled each other, had grown electrified, so sensitive that their fingers seemed to recoil from each other's flesh. Clara cast a sly glance at her mother, who knew nothing of Harry Dana.

She grew aware of a murmur of conversation between Peter and Laura. His voice was strained with effort; her mother's attention seemed elsewhere despite the fixity of her gaze on Peter. He was speaking of a Japanese woman writer with whom he had had lunch the day before. She had brought him a small perfect apple. "How poetic," remarked Laura. They had published her novel a few months ago. It was the best one that had come across his desk in some time.

"Not still another report from the universal crotch?" asked Laura.

"No, no," Peter said quickly. "Not at all. She's serious. It's a good book."

"A money-maker?" asked Desmond and he gave a strange little giggle. "I know what that *serious* means, Peter Rice. No sale, that's what it means."

"Quite right," Peter said lightly.

"There's nothing wrong with making money," Desmond asserted indignantly. Laura laughed. "Well—there isn't!" he protested. "All these *serious* people, they're the biggest fakers of all!"

"I know," Peter agreed. "But this woman isn't a faker." He spoke of other writers, other books, ones that held no interest for him, sales figures to reassure Desmond, bits of gossip to entertain Laura.

But he kept to himself his true disaffection with the world he described with such coolness. It would have shamed him to have revealed to anyone at all his dislike for the work he did in the world, the thing he had come to feel he could do best. He no longer liked to read. The sight of a printed page filled him with a faint but persistent nausea. He read nothing except the manuscripts for which he was responsible. On weekends, he drove miles from the city, staying at an inn if he could find one, but more often at motels where he watched television programs, or, if there was a bar, nursing one drink for hours, or walking in any kind of weather until he was tired enough to sleep. But then, at least, he was away from the ceaseless din of publishing, out of reach of the culture experts, many of whose manuscripts ended up on his desk, and whose juices flowed, he had come to believe, for no other reason than the excitation of maintaining their names in print, who performed, deaf to their own failing voices so like the voices of aged singers, lest they faint into the sickness of anonymity, who could never be still but must add their own noise to the universal screech of opinion, their oppositions or agreements equally meaningless since both were only advertisements of their will to persist. Yet he knew that they were humble and depressed, too, like eternal suitors. They had entrusted their selves to public keeping, they were dependent on the careless, fleeting attention they got. When their books were published, Peter's phone rang constantly, the authors calling, calling—why had they not been reviewed by so-and-so? Why had they been neglected by this one or that one? Why had the publishers placed so few ads in the newspapers, the magazines? Why were their books not in this store or that one? What the hell was the matter with the distributors? Had the salesmen been ordered to ignore their books because their views were unpopular? Unpopular! The public had a mouth so blind and avid it swallowed anything, its jaws frozen open in perpetual appetite. Peter could soothe these authors, reassure them. He was known in his department as "the soother." And somewhere, he felt a fugitive sympathy with them, if only because of his lack of any sympathy whatsoever—and his helplessness—with the newer writers, the ones coming up, with their staged outrageousness and their shrewd grasp of business practices.

"Lunch is the great danger," he was saying. "Do you remember when I was so overweight, Laura?"

"You were never that, you've always been thin," she replied with peculiar emphasis on *thin*, meaning, he guessed, that he had always been dried up.

"It took me years to learn not to order what the writers ordered," he continued. "They're *really* hungry. I have to eat modestly but without giving offense. They're sensitive, they don't wish to appear like hogs. Now, I have a glass of white wine, an omelet, a good deal of black coffee to counterbalance their desserts."

Again, he had caught sight of Clara's nose, that fine narrow ridge, exactly like Ed Hansen's. He wondered if her eyes were the same color as his? Mauve and bluish? But the largeness of her head, her lineless carved lips, her slow, defensive walk, owed nothing to Hansen, everything to Maldonada.

It was Carlos who had introduced him to the Hansens thirty years ago. He had driven with him out to Long Island where Ed was living temporarily in a rented house on Long Island Sound. His arrangements were always temporary—like life, he was fond of saying.

Peter and Carlos had walked through the French doors and found the Hansens in a ramshackle but comfortable living room. It had been a spring day, the room smelled of the unthawed earth and the first fresh greenness outside, of damp rattan furniture and coffee, of the leather harnesses of the two Hansen dogs. Shortly after their arrival, a man had come from the village with a case of liquor and stayed awhile to talk to Ed. Ed was already known in the village. He couldn't bear not being known in a village. In Europe or the United States, he always found villages; they never lived in cities, only visited them. Ed and the delivery man had spoken of the advance of spring, of what fish could be gotten from the waters of the Sound, which rippled placidly just beyond the edge of the ragged neglected garden. The light had been so sweet, so clear! A pale, maidenly light that felt upon Peter's cheeks as if it came from the cool petals of the crocuses that were already fading beyond the French doors but which he could see scattered around the peony plants whose fat, plumlike buds beat out a soundless tattoo when the breeze struck them. He had not known Carlos well, then, and he had never known a Spaniard before. Here were Spaniards. Laura in the light, clear air like a dark root, slender then, balancing her peony head, sitting quietly in a chintz-covered chair, the sunlight falling upon the rug at her feet and on the legs of the white rattan table on the edge of which her cigarette burned. She had said, "I suppose I ought to go and find an ashtray," and smiled at him. He always, in recalling that room, the spring morning, thought that it was there he had experienced the most intense moment of joy, of optimism, in his life, because of Ed Hansen in his English jacket, because of Laura, her long arms crossed over the bodice of her light dress, rising and walking to the kitchen to get an ashtray, smiling at him, because of a sense of endless possibilities hinted at by Ed's cameras in their leather cases, by the piled-up magazines and books, the still unpacked suitcases near the fireplace, because he had thought the Hansens brilliant and thrilling and extraordinary, because the air had never smelled so vividly to him of spring flowers.

A year later, he had married Barbara. Ed had introduced her to him. He had felt he was marrying the Hansens, too; he had wanted to marry them.

He heard himself talking but his voice didn't feel as though it belonged to him. The air was dreadful in this place, with its contrived sentimental restaurant dusk. He started suddenly. Clara had touched his shoulder, but it was Laura who spoke.

"Oh, Peter, come with us!" she said. She spoke with a strange oppressive heaviness like one in a trance. The old hope rose in him that everything was still possible, that he could go back to his apartment and pack a bag and leave it all behind him, the necessity of earning a living—he was no heir—the loneliness of his life. But that hope was a knife that cut him down. He glanced angrily at Laura, then away from her to his own hands that were folding his napkin. She was always trying to get men to get it up! Always arousing them to empty purpose. He was too old to get it up. Then he told himself to calm down; she had spoken to his momentary delusion, but it was his, not hers. He was almost amused by himself, wanting now to explain to Laura how difficult it had become to get it up, for work, for talk, for thought, for showers and meals and bill paying, for keeping himself going from day to day. He only wanted to remain quiet, and allow himself this small indulgence of Laura now and then, a kind of holiday that made him forget for a while the settled, scant half-life he had bargained for and won. The holiday didn't work its old wonders much anymore.

"Why should I do that?" Peter asked with a touch of spite.

Laura looked troubled, not, he knew, by his spite but by his question. *Why* never figured in her sense of things.

"Don't be such a poop!" Desmond said, taking visible pleasure in his coarseness. The pleasure was fleeting. Sourness bubbled in his throat. He would be up half the night, staggering between his bed and the toilet. At some point, Laura would turn on the light and say, with a certain ghastly patience, "Can I get you something?" It was better, he supposed, than it had been in the early days, when she smashed a lamp against a wall or dropped a radio on its face, as though her rage could prevent him from emptying out his guts into the toilet bowl! Yes, it had all gotten much better. Only two to go now, first that tiresome prune of an editor, then Clara. Laura and he would return to their room—perhaps he could sleep right through his dizziness. In the morning, he would order their breakfast, Laura would read him a comic thing or two from the newspaper in a tranquil voice. She would be smoking her cigarette right to the end like a street kid did; he would be packing. He packed wonderfully! He had bought her a present he intended to give her when the boy came for their luggage, a small *papier mâché* Easter egg,

inside it a tiny, perfect village she could peer at through a
hole at one end. She would love that, she loved presents.
He started to grin. He looked at her. She was bent forward,
her hand clenched against her breasts, her face shadowed,
saturnine, utterly unlike the woman of his reverie. Why
was she opposing him? He wanted to shake her.

"I'm not a poop," Peter Rice said pleasantly. "I'm a wage
slave. But next time—perhaps next time . . ."

"Carlos never changes," remarked Desmond irritably.
Laura sat up straight and shook her head.

"Oh, yes. He changes," she said. "We all do, we grow
disfigured and hideous like my poor mother's black shoes."

Instantly, Clara saw the shoes on the floor of their closet
in the Brooklyn apartment. On her one visit to the old people's home, she had observed that Alma wore slippers.
They were exactly like her roommate's, old Mrs. Levy. Mrs.
Levy had skin the texture and color of a water biscuit.
Mrs. Levy was almost always in bed, her slippers on the
floor, side by side like two old tabby cats. She imagined
them asleep at night, the two female bodies motionless beneath institutional blankets. She supposed all the old people wore slippers. But were they permitted to keep one pair
of shoes? In case they were taken out for a stroll? In case
the world changed and they could live among others? Or
for their burial? Or was it that the old were so detestable
that the less noise they made, the better?

Clara feared that a further conversation about age might
lead back to her. If she could only shout, "I don't *know*
why I don't go to see Alma. . . ." Let Laura tell her why!
Let Desmond! She began to speak hastily about an article
she'd read on oppossums. She was full of self-derision as
she heard her own voice rise in feigned enthusiasm, doing

what Alma always had done, beseeching them with animals, pressing up against a deepening chill, ordering their attention, even if it was as artificial as her claim upon it; but she would do anything to hide from Laura the confused, soft, self-accusatory core of her feelings about her grandmother. Now, when the evening was nearly over, she was more alarmed, more alien to herself, than when she had entered the hotel room where the very singularity of her rare meetings with Laura provided a kind of screen against which they could play out a show of sympathy. But the mist had begun to disperse hours ago, when Laura had turned up the hem of her dress revealing to them both Clara's feeble lie. In her lay a vision of a barren landscape and of herself jigging across it, a mortified clown in an empty place.

She grabbed up a serving spoon. "When oppossums are born, you can fit a whole litter of them, five or six, into a spoon like this." Desmond stared torpidly at the spoon. Clara brought it close to her eyes. "Here we are!" she squeaked. Laura burst into laughter.

"Oh, do that again," she cried.

"Here we are!" Clara squeaked more shrilly.

Laura leaned back against her chair and flung back her head. The laughter flowed from her out beyond their table, great waves of wild sound full of such risibility, such gratification, that people all around them turned to look and smile. Desmond sat up excitedly and took Clara's hand that held the spoon and kissed it and he too began to laugh, coughing and patting Clara's arm. Tears were running down Laura's face as she rocked back and forth until, at last, she grew quiet, wiping her eyes with the backs of her hands. "Oh, Clara . . ." she said once, softly, with a curious note of regret.

The unexpected felicity of the moment delivered Peter from memory and brought him smiling into ordinary unconsciousness. The evening *had* been a strain, but they'd all been cooped up so long in that hotel room, city weather was uncomfortable, dreadful, really, one had less protection against it than country weather, and there was certainly a point in one's life—he had reached it some time ago—where tobacco and liquor and rich food were negative pleasures firing one up treacherously only to drop one into the ignominious realization of one's age. And he had talked too much about his work, not just to be diverting but out of a somewhat shady desire to refute what Laura had said earlier in the evening, about his detesting his job, about how people in his office must feel about him. It had rankled.

But something had happened.

Peter looked from Laura to Clara. The young woman was stricken, Laura's mouth was open, her teeth clenched as though in agony, her hands grasping the edge of the table. Desmond's hands were up in the air, the girl was shaking her head violently. Laura was rising—

"You've stolen my voice!" she cried. "You've stolen it . . . I can't bear it another moment . . . I can't. . . ." And she turned away from them, and pushed past waiters and tables and diners to the front of the restaurant where she appeared to hurl herself against the double doors, hurl herself into the street outside.

At the table, there was a stunned silence, then Desmond said dully, "She forgot her fur coat."

"The Spanish secession," Peter said, and regretted it at once.

"But I didn't say *anything*," Clara moaned, clenching her fists and pressing them to her cheeks.

"You must have said something," Clapper snarled.

"But—I didn't!" the girl cried piercingly. "Only all that about the goddamned oppossums—My God! What did I say!"

"She had too much to drink," Peter said quickly, grabbing Clara's hands which now fumbled weakly at the tablecloth. "She was overwrought. There's more to leave-taking than cheerful goodbyes and packed suitcases. I could see she was distressed—it wasn't your fault—don't be foolish—"

"Shut up!" exclaimed Clapper, seizing the sugar bowl as though he intended to fling it at someone. Clara stood up, stared at them with an expression of unutterable woe, and left without a word. At the checkroom, she stopped and dug into her bag until she found her cardboard tag. As the woman laid her coat across the counter, Clara saw her mother's fur coat, resplendent, on a hanger. She would carry it to Laura. But what if Laura didn't go back to the hotel? Clara couldn't take the coat; she might never get rid of it. And as she moved through the doors, her heart beating violently, sunk with hopelessness, she remembered where that coat had come from, from that wealthy South American relative of the Maldonadas who owned mines and grew orchids, who had kept a New York apartment on the east side of the city for his business visits, a penthouse, empty save a few days every year, but cleaned twice weekly by an elderly Finnish woman. She had seen him once, heard him telephone Berlin, then London. He had

offered her a plate of dried fruit and had smiled unpleas-
antly when she'd refused any. He had been a small, plump
man with dyed black hair and tapering, narrow fingers and
he spoke to her in a corrosive, hectoring Spanish. Someone had told her last year that he had jumped out of a
window and killed himself. And Laura had, she had said in
one of those harrowing admissions of hers, "gone to bed"
with him. "Let me tell you how I got that coat," she had
said. And then, "I'm terrible. Am I not? I was so tired of
not having anything." And she had shaken her head as
though marveling. "I seem to be capable of anything," she
had said.

The rain had not abated. If Laura wasn't in her room,
Clara told herself she would wait in the lobby until her
mother appeared. She didn't know what she would do
then. Perhaps something had really happened, at last. It
was this sense of a new turn, wrenching everything out of
its habitual place, an intimation of another way of being,
that must account for the sudden lightening of her spirit,
and an eerie joy as though she were about to be delivered
from prophecy into chance.

When Clara was six, her father had taken her from
Alma's to see Laura in another of the Hansens' borrowed
apartments in New York where they were stopping a few
days. In the empty living room, Ed had stood with his
fingers to his lips, warning her to be silent as though
someone were sleeping. He had led her to a couch where
she had sat. At once, an enormous dog had loped in from
another room, gone directly toward her, and leaped to the
couch and sat beside her panting faintly, evenly. Then she
had looked up and seen Laura standing in a doorway,
holding a glass in which ice cubes floated, looking at her.

It was as though a stone had looked at her. Suddenly, Laura had hurled the glass into the room. There had been no crash—it must have landed somewhere but something, rug or curtain, had muffled the sound. Clara had crouched beside the dog, and it seemed to her now she had been crouched all these years, waiting for the smash of glass as someone who has been made aware through a mute show that she has been accused awaits an explication.

It was more bearable to be charged—even if grotesquely charged—with voice-stealing than with the irreducible fact of her existence. But how could she help it if her voice was like her mother's? She thought, then, of Harry Dana's objection to how she *sounded* when she spoke of Laura. Perhaps there had been a grain of truth in Laura's accusation. Clara spoke aloud as though on a telephone: "Hello? Hello. Is that you, Harry?" and hearing in her own voice the very intonation of Laura's, was so startled, she laughed in self-deprecation, in chagrin, yet feeling an odd kind of triumph.

"Hello, yourself," said a man who had stopped to look at her. The collar of his coat was held tight by an enormous safety pin.

She hurried on toward the hotel whose entrance she could see now a half block away. An overturned litter basket lay against the curb, evidence, perhaps, of Laura's passage. The trouble is, she thought, I believe no one but Laura.

A postprandial calm had descended upon the lobby. A few people sat dozing in the dimness. Clara went up to the Clappers' room. She passed the now silent, closed rooms where Randy Cunny had made her literary debut. A paper cup lay on the floor, all that was left. No one answered her knock. She listened for a long time, her ear pressed against the door. If Laura was in there, she was playing dead. It was unlikely. She was not given to sulking. What was likely was that she was flinging herself recklessly about the rainy streets, in a state of exalted outrage, an abandon that Clara almost envied, like the abandon of a dancer in a frenzy of pure movement, mind sunk into body.

In the lobby, she found a chair sheltered by a plastic plant and half hidden from the reception desk. Across from her, at the other end of the room, a great mirror hung from the wall, its frame a thick plaited design in gilt. She could see, reflected in it, a shadow that must be herself, and other shadows, undifferentiated, ambiguous, moving indolently back and forth. And she thought of Alma's story of how she had glimpsed herself in a mirror for the first time in her life when she was a week or two past her sixteenth birthday, a story of such limpid innocence that Clara had hardly believed it, yet reverberating with the echoes of an era, a class, a way of living gone forever. One Sunday morning while she was cooking the Sunday dinner, Alma had told Clara about it, happy at the beginning of the day in her unavailing illusion that the end of the day would somehow be different this time.

In Havana, she had been met by her bridegroom's cousin, La Señora Gonzaga, whom she had never met before. The journey from Spain, during which her sixteenth year had passed with the waves, had been arduous. She knew nothing of where she was going, of Cuba, of cousins, of her husband-to-be whose tintype she had become more afraid to look at with each day that passed on the sea. Then came the journey by land to the plantation, accompanied by this small, austere woman who often told her to sit with more "restraint" or to talk with less haste, and above all to breathe with more delicacy, less excitement—one should not be heard breathing.

The first thing she had noticed at the plantation were the stocks in which the slaves were punished, and she had exclaimed at their ugliness. La Señora had warned her that she must not notice such things. She did not discover what they were for until months later. She was taken through great silent rooms, up the broad, curving stairway to a room larger than the salon of her parents' house in Barçelona. There was a strange, bitter, piercing smell everywhere—it seemed green to her, like the new bitter green leaves of spring. She was to rest; the coverlet of a huge bed had been turned back by a young maid who smiled at her as she helped her off with her clothes but would say nothing. When she had been left alone, she had gone to the wide windows. The fields of sugar cane spread as far as her eyes could see, unmoving in the windless air of late afternoon. The fan-shaped leaves of the royal palms in the garden seemed monstrous to her, unnatural. Although nothing stirred, the purpling sky was full of silent violence, the dusk a great wing spreading, shutting out all that was familiar in her life, the old far heavens of her childhood that was barely over.

When it was dark, servants had brought her a gown, carrying it tenderly as though it were an invalid. She was dressed, her hair piled on top of her head, and last, she was given an ivory fan upon which a parade of brilliant peacocks thinned or widened with the motion of her fingers. The two maids parted from her at the door of the room. She looked down a long gallery; at its end was the staircase. She heard a murmur of many voices rising from the floor below. He would be there too, Señor Maldonada. What on earth was she to say to him? How would she address him? But she moved lightly down the gallery toward her fate. She had an inquiring nature; unlike her sisters, she was full of questions. She saw, coming toward her down the long reach, a girl so beautiful that she had begun to smile with shyness and pleasure. She held her fan to her lips. The girl did the same. She realized it was herself, reflected in a large pier glass at the end of the hall. So she had traveled that unimaginable distance, sent on her way by a marriage pact in which she had no say, suffering the first violations of her privacy in the confines of the small ship, only to discover the reality of her person, glimpsed fully for the first time on the eve of her marriage to an unknown man of thirty-eight.

Clara stood up watching the blur of her movement of rising in the mirror. She looked only for an instant at her reflection, then bowed her head and left the hotel. It was futile to wait for Laura. What would they be able to say to each other? It was better to go home. When the Clappers returned from their trip, she would see them again; nothing would be said about this evening. It would be as if it had never happened. Clara had other things to think about. Tomorrow, she planned to take the day off from work. She was driving to New Jersey with Harry, who had a client there. It was the first chance they'd had to spend so much time together.

In the restaurant, Peter Rice was defending himself against Desmond's sullen accusations.

"I didn't do anything," he protested angrily. "You know

that I didn't. You also know how Laura interrupts her own boredom—of course, she doesn't pay any mind to anything but her own mood. That's why she's our darling. It's that girl you ought to be concerned about—"

"That girl can take care of herself!" exclaimed Desmond. "What are you babbling about her for? She's used to it. She'd better be. But I'm the one that will have a night of it. Laura won't cool off till I get her in that cabin tomorrow. I'm the one that *sees* to Laura. All of you just sit around and *watch* her."

"All of what? There's hardly one of us left alive!" Peter erupted into outraged, noisy laughter. Clapper shook his arm.

"Stop it. Please stop it!" he begged. "My life with Laura absolutely exhausts me!"

Without liking Clapper any better, Peter felt a faint touch of sympathy for him. Then Desmond saw the bill the waiter had left. He snatched it up and held it close to his face, his eyes narrowed, his mouth tight with suspicion as he added up the figures.

"Let me take care of half of it," Peter offered. Desmond shot him a glance of utter derision.

"Come off it," he grunted. "This is my party."

Laura had long since passed the entrance to the hotel. She had been running then, in a transport of rage, aware with bitter pleasure that the people on the sidewalk were making way for her, afraid of her, a coatless, rain-soaked fury, her teeth chattering with cold.

That girl! That girl with her open mouth, her idiot fearfulness—and Peter Rice, an insect husk, the goddamned vampire sucking her life away, that bloodless Christian sewing machine with his intolerable daintiness—what had *she* to do with such creatures, what did she have to do with thick-witted, thick-ankled old Desmond and his infant thieving of liquor, or with debauched Carlos—but at the thought of Carlos, Laura began to cry. She didn't understand *anything!* The unyielding mystery of her impulses was punishment enough for whatever she had done—she thought she had put them to sleep so long ago, that they had withered away just as she was withering away, but they were awake, the old beasts of her life, so merciless, so cruel. She sobbed aloud, feeling her wretched hair pasted to her cheeks, the waves all gone now—she desperately needed to use a toilet—she felt she couldn't speak to a living soul, that she was cut off forever from speech, that if she spoke, there would be no words, only a barbaric gibbering, that there was no language for the torment of what she was feeling, of her aloneness. But she wanted no one! Only animal presences, a dog watching her silently, a cat suddenly standing up, its paws resting on a windowsill, to follow the flight of a bird. The utter quietness of animal being, that slow sinking into the eternal present that was animal sensibility, and she remembered how she had once undone a knotted string in front of a lion's cage in a zoo, never looking at the lion, fully aware of its interest as she slowly untied the string, she and the lion, rapt, inside the unity of their attention, alive in that moment in such a peculiar, ultimate way. Ed had loved what she'd done; he hadn't believed her when she said she knew she could catch and hold the attention of a lion.

Lions! She had been going on a long journey to Africa!

An enormous grief rose in her. The knowledge of the

death of her mother flooded her bloodstream, entered her bowels, her marrow. She felt she was about to urinate on the street—her bladder was giving way—that nothing stood between her now and a leaking away of her life. She tried to imagine the black-toned, echoing clang of the bells of Campostella, that clanging from the void itself. Then she saw the blue flicker of a neon sign that read: *Bar*.

Clutching her arms around her purse which she held to her chest, she pushed open the door into a dark room, and without glancing at anyone, made for the back, for the door which said: *Little Girls*. She heard the choking flush of a toilet, and just made it into the empty one of two cubicles. She groaned with relief, her arms across her knees, the wet purse sliding onto the tile floor. Still, she wept and coughed. But she told herself that, at least, she had not had to watch Desmond pay the bill. It was always offensive.

CHAPTER FOUR

The Messenger

Desmond was nearly sober. His body was an affliction now; he would not be all right until after he had slept. But he couldn't fall on his bed and bury himself beneath the blankets. He must wait for Laura. He had to suffer what sleep would have spared him. A chambermaid had turned down the covers of the beds and carried off the empty bottles and glasses. The room still smelled of tobacco. Desmond drank several glasses of water. Once, he retched violently and heard himself moan, "Don't!"

He was unable to open the window more than a crack. He opened the door to the corridor and leaned against it until he had aired out the room.

He went to the desk and spread out the paraphernalia of the trip, passports, tickets, vouchers of various kinds. He read the fine print on train schedules, then spread out the plan of the ship, his mind blank. On the honeycomb plan of the ship, he had already marked their cabin. He put his finger on the cross he had made, felt a sudden flutter of his heart, and felt cowardly and weak and confused.

Half an hour or so passed. The air in the room was chilled without being fresh. He had forgotten to close the

window. On the inside cover of his passport, there was a
space to write down next of kin. He supposed he'd better
put Carlos down for that. His own parents were dead; he
had no sisters, no brothers. No one. There was Ellie. But
Laura would not care for his putting his daughter's name
down. And he had no real interest in her—it might be a
dismal fact, but it was true.

At 10:30, he changed into a bathrobe. Where was his
flask? He rummaged around in a handcase, remembering
he had filled the flask two days ago when Laura had gone
to say goodbye to her mother. It was a silver flask engraved
with his initials, given to him years ago by a girl whose
name and face he could not recall. He found it, unscrewed
the top, and took a large swallow. God! What renewal!
What relief! His sense of his own substance returned to
him. But he mustn't have anymore. Oh—he knew all the
subtle trickery of alcohol!

The room was really cold. He took Laura's robe from the
closet and lay it across her bed. He packed away all the
books Peter Rice had brought except for the one he
thought she might like to start reading, even tonight. He
knew her so well—she could read through anything, a cat-
aclysm, even one of her own making. He had selected a
detective story. He opened it to the first page: "Inspector
Guthorn was savoring his second cup of China tea when
the telephone—" He put the book down on her night table.

Laura would not telephone. Until she was over it, whatever it was, she would not remember what telephones
were for. Through the open bathroom door, he caught
sight of her fur coat which he had hung up on the shower
curtain rod. It had enraged him to carry the coat through
the streets from the restaurant. He would like to have

dropped it in a gutter. But still, it was worth a bit. He went and shook it. The fur was still damp from the rain. He caught a discreet animal smell. Expensive. When he'd slapped the check for the coat down on the counter, he'd forgotten to tip the coatroom girl. But he couldn't go back into the restaurant. He walked along in the rain, clutching that goddamned coat, hating his life.

The matter of the coat, where she had gotten it, was a closed question. She had told him it had been given to her by an elderly relative whose wife had died. He hadn't quite believed her. But he didn't know what else to believe. Even years ago, when she'd gotten the coat, she'd been too old to receive that kind of gift from a lover.

He noticed the newspaper folded on a chair. He looked up the shipping news and found the name of their ship and its sailing time.

There was a sound at the door. He went toward it quickly. It was a fumbling, rustling sound like that of someone pressing along the wall in a dark room. He started to open the door, then leaned against it.

"Laura?"

He heard a low cry. "Is it you?" he asked. It might be a drunken woman, or two people, accomplices come to rob him.

"Let me in!"

He opened the door. Laura stood there shuddering, her head bowed. He threw his arm around her hunched shoulders and instantly his arm was wet. She was soaked through. Clots of her wet hair touched his neck.

He took her to the bathroom and undressed her, then took a towel and rubbed her down as though he were currying a horse. He was happy, saved. He removed her shoes, pressed her gently to the toilet seat and rubbed her feet. Then he left her for a moment and went to get the flask. But when he held it to her lips, her eyes flashed open and she seized the flask and flung it on the tiled bathroom floor. She began to moan. He heard words. But they were Spanish words! Oh, Christ! Not that!

He lifted up her head. Her eyes were closed, her jaws rigid beneath his fingers.

"What is it?" he cried.

"My mother is dead," she whispered. "She's dead. . . ."

Her head fell against his belly; her moans were like a rumbling in his stomach. He stared at the wall. He didn't understand what she'd said. The word *dead* had clacked like colliding billiard balls, a word of wood, the two hard consonants clapped against each other.

He half lifted her and led her into the bedroom, to the bed, then got her into her bathrobe. She sat there, on the edge of the bed, caved in, her damp hair in spikes, moaning. For a second, he loathed her.

He found her slippers and pushed her feet into them. He noticed her toes were red and swollen. It was the city shoes. In the country, she went around in soft canvas shoes. He tried to press her down; sitting up she was peculiarly threatening, like a statue about to topple over and crush him. But she fought him off and remained precariously upright.

"We have to tell Eugenio and Carlos," she said. She looked up at him, and then repeated what she had said very slowly.

"But—how do you know?"

"The home called, this afternoon just when we got back."

"But, Laura! You didn't tell them, Carlos, Clara . . ."

She was silent.

"You didn't tell *me*."

She covered her eyes with her hands.

"Don't do that!"

Now she fell back on her bed, staring up at the ceiling.

"Why?" His voice faltered on that word. He remembered that when they'd come back that afternoon, Laura had gone to the elevator, saying, "Darling . . . come on, come on . . ." and so he had merely glanced at the message the desk clerk had handed him, seen it was only the home which had telephoned, old Alma, probably, wanting to say *adios* another hundred times, thinking to tell her later, she could always call her mother in the morning and say goodbye then. . . .

"Why?" he asked again, thinking he would have to go through his pockets, find that message and throw it away.

"It was mine," she whispered. He couldn't stand the senselessness of what she had said.

"Your what?" he asked brusquely.

"Mine!" she said again. "They don't deserve—I wouldn't give Carlos the pleasure . . ."

Desmond started. Pleasure! She must have meant relief. He did not intend to pursue it. He wasn't obliged to understand everything Laura said. Sometimes he felt he lived the life of a waiter. In this instance—it wasn't a tragedy, after all, the death of an old woman—he was the one who had long ago taken care of the business end of death, buying the plot, giving the deed to the home, signing papers. It was he who freed Laura from official life. A year or two ago she had said, after he had returned from the home, "Don't tell me what you did. Don't say a word."

Something his ex-wife had said to him years before occurred to him now. His own parents had died in the same year. They had both been buried in a cemetery near the Boston suburb in which they had lived the last years of their lives. Each time he had returned to New York, he had found himself unable to explain to his friends why he had been away. It was the former Mrs. Clapper who had announced their deaths. "You seem to feel you've been abased by your parents passing away," she had said to him. How he had hated that "passing away!" But perhaps there had been something in what she'd said. The word *pleasure* rang on softly in his mind. Relief, pleasure, abasement. But loss and grief? He quailed inwardly at the thought of those regions of feeling; for a moment, he sensed his own stubborn narrowness. He sensed it without introspection, in the same way someone might observe to himself that he has lied, but then, like a provincial angered by a fleeting vision of a larger world, he began to belittle that world. People were only concerned with themselves. He felt a bitter disappointment.

"Well—there goes the trip," he said.

"The trip?" she asked. She began to weep again.

"Well—postponed, then," he said appeasingly.

"I told them the funeral is to be tomorrow," she said. "In the end, she's to be buried overnight, like a Jew."

"Don't you want to tell Carlos and Clara and Eugenio?"

She groaned. "Help me!" she cried out. "Help me . . . I don't know what I'm to do."

He was frantic suddenly. She looked so heavy lying there. What if he had to lift her, to dress her, to make her walk?

"You don't have to do anything!" he exclaimed.

"I hated it," she gasped out. "The going on and on—she's always been there, waiting for me to do something about her, about her life. What could I have done? Oh, God! Do you remember what I told you? How she used to go off and just leave us? Disappear for days, and the neighbors would feed us?"

He couldn't bear the dazed look on her face, but her eyes gleamed at him—he felt the way she was straining toward something, straining as though she would burst.

"When she came back, we could hear her singing to herself in the kitchen. Didn't she *know* she'd been away? Clucking to herself, singing, saying we were out of olive oil, kissing us, kissing us while we shrank from her face, her hands, not one of us able to ask her where she'd been, not knowing till years later she'd gone to stay with that old bitch, Gonzaga, in her suite at the Plaza . . . oh, we always knew when she'd gone when we came home from school, we could feel the emptiness of the house and the three of us would sit in the living room, trying to decide where we could go for supper, and we all spoke Spanish then, when we were alone, never in front of the neighbors who might give us a meal, who shook their heads over us and pitied us, and we were thinking about what they'd give us to eat, and whether this time she'd never come back. . . ."

"Don't, Laura. Stop. You'll make yourself ill. But I don't understand how you went through this evening without saying anything. I mean, if you'd told me!"

She was sitting up, clutching the blanket to her chin, sniffling and looking around wildly. He felt trapped himself among the relentlessly stingy amenities of the hotel room.

"I couldn't," she said despairingly. "I couldn't have
borne it, seeing their dismay that they'd have to *do* something. And I wanted, this once, to be the only one, the only
one who knew. . . ."

"I guess it doesn't matter . . ." he said, his voice trailing
off.

"But she didn't leave Clara," Laura said. "She never left
Clara." She suddenly grabbed his hand, then dropped it as
though repelled, as though it were useless. "My mother was
so innocent. All her life, she refused to *know* what life is."

"I'll phone Carlos," he said.

"No!" she cried. "Not on the phone. I don't want to hear
it on the phone. And he won't answer if he's got someone
there. Someone has to go to both of them, to him and
Eugenio."

"I don't want to leave you."

"You can't leave me!"

"Shall I call Clara? Ask her to go to them?"

"No!" her voice rang out. "Not her! She's not to know!"

He started to protest, but she looked at him with such
animus that he drew away from her. He stood up and went
to the windows, thinking, she's gone over the edge.

"Call Peter Rice," she said. "He'll go and find them, tell
them."

"Yes," he said gratefully.

Peter answered after the fifth ring. Desmond told him
shortly why he was calling. Then, although he had meant
to say that they had just heard the news of Alma's death,
he heard himself tell the truth. But there was no reason to
lie; it wasn't anyone's business to inquire why Laura had
suppressed the news all that evening. He heard Peter's
sharp intake of breath, his disbelieving "You mean, she

knew in the afternoon?" and Desmond said quickly, "That isn't the point. The point is, I can't very well leave her alone right now. So if you could go to them, you know Eugenio lives behind his office? And then to Carlos—"

"What about Clara?" interrupted Peter.

"Clara is not—," Desmond began, but Laura grabbed the phone from his hand and held it to her ear. She seemed to listen for a minute, then she said tonelessly, "Clara is not to be told. She wouldn't be interested."

She handed the telephone back to Desmond instantly. He heard nothing. "Are you there?" he asked.

"I'm here," Peter said faintly.

Desmond gave him Eugenio's address. Peter knew where Carlos lived.

"We're awfully grateful to you," he said. "You can imagine—" But Peter had hung up. It was done.

"We'll have to collect her things. I don't know what we'll do with them. Do you think the home would take care of that? She didn't have much."

He took her hand again, and this time she let it rest between his hands. They were quiet, looking at each other. At last she said, "I'm sorry about the trip."

"It's only a postponement."

"I'm sorry about everything, the way I ran out tonight. I don't know what happened. I don't even remember now what it was."

He brought her hand to his lips and kissed it.

"Mamá had an awful life."

He nodded, the sense of her words barely touching him. He was moved by the softening of her features, the quietness in her face that belonged only to him, to the privacy between them.

"Desmond. She was such a beautiful young girl."

"I know."

"She never knew it. She never knew what she was at any time in her life. She had an idea about submission, you see. She submitted to everyone—it was being good. Listen . . . I'm glad she died. I'm glad it is over for her."

Of course, he understood now what she meant. Everyone is glad when the old die. Glad is entirely different from pleasure. She hadn't meant that. Laura told the truth—whatever it was at the moment. He could be glad with her. It was better for the old, all of them straggling and straying down the halls of the home like old, old dogs, stunned with age and infirmity, waiting for nothing.

"I understand what you mean," he said eagerly.

She gave him an exceedingly somber look.

"I don't think you do," she said.

CHAPTER FIVE

The Brothers

At night in the city, things were never invisible, always somewhat visible, as though lurking. There was no utter black night in the city. Day drained away; darkness came diluted by a pale but ruthless artificial light. Should a sleeper wake suddenly, there would be no surcease from seeing. Peter Rice, his hand still resting on the telephone whose ringing had snatched him out of his brief sleep, stood in his living room, his pajama bottoms twisted around his waist, his bare feet chilled on the floor. Light from the street revealed the shadowed clumps of his possessions. Reluctantly, he went to turn on his own lights, one next to a bookcase, one near an easy chair, and one hanging from the ceiling over a small round table where he ate his meals.

As the room revealed itself, one, two, three, it had a certain novelty; it was his yet for a moment he was not of it. Of personal things, there were only two. One was a sketch by Ed Hansen hanging on the wall near the door that led to Peter's study. It was a drawing Ed had made of Peter and Barbara a few months after their marriage. They had been sitting on the ground, leaning against the trunk of an apple tree. Barbara's hand was resting on his knee. He was looking away from her, out of the picture. Near one of the living room windows was a child's white wicker rocking chair that had belonged to Peter's grandmother. It was the only thing he had taken for himself from the Rice house when he and his sisters had emptied it out before putting it up for sale. On his grandmother's eighty-third birthday, she had shown him she could still sit in the chair. Often, when his glance fell upon it, he remembered the old woman crowing victoriously as she rocked, her arthritic fingers resting upon the wicker arms, cake crumbs from her birthday cake clinging to her upper lip. He had had to help her up out of it and she had fallen against him. He never forgot the feel of her aged body, so breakable, like an armful of dry twigs. Beside the chair, on the floor, was a pot holding a large, straggling plant. It had been given to Peter by his neighbor downstairs, Violet Darcy. The Darcys lived in the duplex of the town house on 11th Street of which Peter occupied the top floor. Violet had said he needed something green and growing in his life, something to take care of. When the soil in the pot got dry and crusty, he felt like a torturer. He wished it would die. But it continued to send out shoots and new leaves which turned yellow in a short time and dropped off to the floor. It was an ugly, shapeless plant and he wondered why he didn't kill it. When he opened the door to his apartment, it was always the first thing he saw.

It was just past midnight. He had been asleep little more than an hour. He drank a glass of water in his small kitchen, then went to get dressed. When the phone had rung, he had thought it was Violet calling. Abject, and apologetic, she had called him once or twice quite late when her older child, Gina, who had just turned eighteen, had not come home. "Her love life is her own business," Violet would avow with a strained but insistent leniency, "but I don't want her murdered in the streets." It was to Peter, the last few years, that she turned for reassurance. He never said much; if he listened long enough, Violet always talked herself out of her apprehensions. Peter knew that Mr. Darcy, an advertising executive, had no patience with Violet's worries about their children. He was a tall, muscular man who entered into and departed from rooms quickly, athletically, as though following a secret program of body building. Peter had known them for ten years. He and Violet were friends of a sort; he and Mr. Darcy were polite to each other. Violet frequently spoke of the goodness of her husband's heart but he seemed to Peter glacially cold, animated by the hostile conviction that he was a sensible man in a world of fools. He had many opinions, and he delivered them like short, hard blows. There was no hue of personal feeling in what he said; he never conversed. Their younger child, Roger, a boy of fourteen, had a cowed, hopeless look. When Mr. Darcy was darting about their home with his intense physical irritability like a wasp's, Peter had overheard Roger whispering to himself the names of various car makes. A magic incantation? But Peter had long given up speculating about the inner life of the Darcys. He and Violet were fond of each other; she diverted him from his own fretfulness. Sometimes he was ashamed—it was hardly friendship, this mindless feeding on someone else's personality, yet he was truly grateful to her; she asked very little of him.

He often stopped by for a drink or coffee. She played baroque organ music on her phonograph for him, thinking he liked it. They spoke of the end of the world—perhaps the Chinese were better off, after all. "The Chinese are Oriental idiots," Mr. Darcy had remarked. Violet had no time to read fiction, she said. She read philosophy. She watered herself with philosophy as she watered the plants with which her living room was webbed and leafed and made bosky. She would crook a finger at Peter. Smiling, she would place her hand beneath the limp petal of a flower—"Bloomed just this morning," she would say, "a miracle!" But for all her care, her greenery was scraggly. Among the plain red pots out of which they sent their tendrils and leaves, Violet lingered with her long-spouted watering can as in a lunatic forest dream.

When Peter had moved into his apartment, ten years ago, Violet's kitchen had been covered with posters. First there had been Black Power posters, then leafy cartoons which proclaimed that war was not good for children, then a large photograph of a hirsute poet carrying a placard which read, "Pot is a reality kick," then handsome, lifeless photographs of meadows and woods whose captions asked, "Is our priceless heritage to be destroyed? Our green to go?"

These depthless, transient seizures of sociological or political fashion reflected on Violet's pale brow like the reflections of automobile lights on Peter's bedroom wall as the cars paused at traffic lights, then passed on. The time of posters was gone. Just as the time for introducing Peter to marriageable women had gone. But, he supposed, Violet still wondered what he had in the way of carnal delight. There had been a brief period when she had clearly reached a conclusion about him. It was then she had spoken about homosexuality as though it were a special grace.

In her efforts to reassure him of the infinite range of what consenting adults could consent to as far as *she* was concerned, she spoke in the now conventional language—inane, brutal and mawkish—of sexual matters. He could tell she thought she was being outrageous; he could only guess how she was violating her private sensibilities. What could they be? What were his? He had been celibate a long time. Celibacy was the condition of his whole life. Something had simply stopped in him. It wasn't there anymore. Like his grandmother, he too had become an armful of dry, cold twigs. But he suffered dreadfully sometimes and thought he would prefer outright revulsion against the flesh than this intensifying chill, this spreading pallor of feeling.

Violet loved, and constantly used, certain words—*impalpable, nebulous, indescribable*. It thrilled her to use them; they set the echoes flying; she was rapt as she gave each syllable intense emphasis. Peter was no longer irritated by her fondness for enigmatic language. He had come to believe that Violet was lost in her life—that she was, to herself, nebulous, indescribable, and that Darcy's success in his field, the increasing materiality of their life, the tokens of which she constantly derided, aggravated to the point of terror her sense of her human vulnerability, of the perilous world into which she would be compelled to release her children.

She and Peter did not speak of such things, yet he recognized those spots of fear that broke out in her like the buboes of a hidden plague. It was a kind of payment to her for her interest in him, her concern for him, this recognition and acceptance of what she would not accept in herself.

As he turned out the lights in his living room, he wondered if Violet could hear him moving about above her at such a late hour. Once, wearied by her obsessive cultural affectations, he had thought to introduce her to Laura. What a thought! What malice!

He passed Violet's door, and fought down an impulse to ring her bell, wake her, tell her about the message of death he had to carry, tell her that the dead woman's grandchild was not to be told. It would only have frightened Violet. But, he thought, it frightens me, too.

He continued down the stairs, walking softly, his front door key already in his hand. Sitting on the last step, her legs stretched out beneath the hall table, was Gina Darcy. She was very still, hunched over. Her long brown hair hung lank across the shoulders of her denim jacket. She didn't turn as he neared her and she made no effort to make room for him to pass. He held the banister to prevent himself from falling.

"Gina?"

"Yuh."

She was holding the brown butt of what looked like a hand-rolled cigarette.

"Are you okay?" he asked lightly. He supposed she'd been sitting there some time, smoking marijuana by herself. She slowly turned her thin face up toward him.

"Okay? Yuh. I'm okay."

"On your way home?" he asked foolishly.

She smiled mirthlessly. "Where I am, it's home," she said. "And oddly enough, I *am* home. This is home, isn't it?"

"Yes, it is."

"How about you? You going home?"

"Out," he said shortly.

"Out. In. We're all going home," she said.

He unlocked the door, then hesitated. "Well—ultimately," he said.

"Shit," she said bleakly.

"Good-night," he said, and went out.

Eugenio's office was on Fifth Avenue, around 15th Street, Peter guessed. He turned up his collar and began to walk uptown. Even though it was still raining heavily, there were people about. But there always were people about. A police car passed him. In its window, he glimpsed a long black sideburn on a dead white cheek. Suddenly, the spiraling wail of the siren started up. The car made a U-turn and sped away. Three young black men were walking toward him. They seemed suspended from their enormous spheres of hair. One carried a portable radio out of which issued a hermaphroditic shriek of lament and fury. To this sound, the young man moved his feet several steps back, then forward. Each time his dance separated him from his companions, they waited patiently, silently, until he again closed ranks with them.

He saw by the numbers on the stores and apartment houses that he was close to Eugenio's office, and in a few steps he came to a halt in front of a plate glass window behind which were displayed travel folders and one large airline poster. A faint light emanated from somewhere in the rear of the narrow room. The door was bolted and a shade was half drawn over the glass window. He knocked, softly at first, then more insistently. The light from the back broadened. Nothing happened for a minute, then, very slowly, the shade was raised. Eugenio looked out at him. In one hand, he was holding a threaded needle, in the other a jacket against which his thumb was pressing a button. Eugenio looked puzzled, then recollection came. He stuck the needle into the jacket, retreated for an instant, dropped the jacket on a desk, then returned to unbolt the door.

"Eugenio, it's Peter Rice."

"Yes, Oh, yes. I recognized you. It's been some time. Yes. Quite a while."

"I have to speak with you. May I come in?"

"Of course, of course," Eugenio said with a smile and an accent Peter remembered at once though he had not seen him for some years. The smile had something embarrassed, wary about it. His accent was almost imperceptible, yet it was there, in the curious emphasis he gave to certain words as though he were striking them off like medals.

"I suppose you've heard that I live—I have space back there, you see, behind this office," he said, leading the way. He seemed uneasy about keeping his back to Peter and half turned as he moved along. Peter saw there was only one desk in the office, a few racks of travel folders, one large poster of a castle taped to the wall.

"Rents are so atrocious," Eugenio continued as he stood back to let Peter precede him into a small room. "These landlords are so avaricious, so *predacious*. So I make the best of things, you see. But it's not *grand*."

Suddenly, he dashed back into the office section, returning with the jacket in his hands.

"A little sewing—I had lost a button earlier today, you see. In the subway. And had great good luck in the five-and-ten-cent-store, finding an almost identical button. One

can't hope to find the *same* one of course, not in the five-
and-ten. Won't you sit down?"

The room's small window was barred. A basin, sup-
ported by discolored pipes, jutted out from the wall. Near it
was a couch, a brown blanket folded at one end. A
straight-backed chair stood next to a wrought iron standing lamp. A two-burner hot plate took up most of the surface of a small table. Next to it was a box of salt and a
glass holding several pieces of flatware. A suitcase in a
corner served as another table. A few books were piled on
top of it along with a manila legal folder tied with several
lengths of string. A metal contrivance of the sort Peter had
seen used to hold coats at parties held Eugenio's sparse
wardrobe, a coat, a jacket of some dark material, a blue
suit, the gray pants of the suit jacket on which he was at
present sewing a button. Peter took the other chair, a kind
of folding stool. Behind it was a narrow door which, he as-
sumed, led to a toilet.

"Not very grand," murmured Eugenio once more. "But
then, beggars can't be choosers." He laughed, a grinding
metallic chuckle.

"How are you?" asked Peter, his voice thickened with
the withheld news, knowing there was no way to say what
he had to say except plainly, wishing it would burst out of
him like a shout.

"How am I? Let me see . . . but—your coat. Do let me
hang it up for you. No? Are you sure? Well—I am pleased,
of course, to have company. Although I was *alarmed* when
I heard your knock."

He began to stitch on his button. "You will excuse me if
I go ahead with my work, won't you? Appearance is every-

thing. If one of my customers saw me with a loose button, she might cancel her flight to Cairo—a lucrative fare for the airline company, and a few pennies to me. These rich old women! Alarmed, I was saying. You know, I suppose, that the streets are filled with roaming hyenas these days. Hyenas . . . By the time the police come, one is a *corpse*. So I am rather nervous that one of these hyenas will break down my door. I was tempted to put a sign in the window saying *I have nothing*. But, of course, that would only *incite* them. They aren't really interested in robbery, you see. They are interested in murdering. Imagine having a cannon on one's premises—one that could be moved into place at night. Then, when they attack the door—Boom! Quite a surprise, don't you think?" He ground out another short laugh. "But tell me, you're great friends with my sister, aren't you? Have you seen her lately?"

"Eugenio. I have serious news. Laura sent me to tell you that your mother died this afternoon in the home."

The jacket fell from Eugenio's hands, the needle sticking up out of the button. He was still, his eyes half closed. Then he picked up the jacket and pulled the needle through. He bent his head over his work and said nothing. Outside, the traffic seemed to have stopped. There was no noise except the infinitesimal click of needle against button.

"I'm sorry," said Peter.

Eugenio raised his head. "Would you like something to drink?" he asked. "I can offer you a cup of that dreadful instant coffee or tea. I have no liquor. I don't drink liquor."

"Nothing, thank you."

"Of what?"

Peter looked at him bewildered.

"Of what did she die?"

"They didn't tell me."

"Where is my sister?"

"They're staying at a hotel. They were going to take a ship tomorrow, a tour to Africa."

"Oh? And when are they embarking?"

"They've postponed their trip, or will be postponing it. I'm certain. Because the funeral—"

"I see. I wonder if they used a travel agent? I could have taken care of it for them, the arrangements. I could have made it cheaper. Of course, my sister's husband doesn't have to worry about money. Do you know what time this afternoon?"

"What time she died?" Peter asked, detesting him. "No, I don't know. When you call in the morning about the funeral, you can find out the particulars."

"Yes, the particulars. Do you know my sister never *mentioned* this trip of theirs to me? I didn't even know they were leaving the country." He drew his thread through the fabric, then bit it off with his teeth.

"My mother always warned me not to bite thread," he said. "She thought it was very bad for teeth. Did you know my mother?"

"I met her years ago when Laura and Ed Hansen were still married."

"Edward Hansen. A *remarkable* man. What a charming man! He could charm *anyone*." Eugenio squeezed his eyes shut, his forehead wrinkled, the strange, wary smile appeared on his lips, he shook his head. "No one who had not met him could *imagine* such charm," he said. He looked so wolfish, so oddly triumphant in his appreciation of Hansen.

"I remember," Peter said without emphasis. He was confounded by Eugenio's reception of the news. He didn't know what to do with Eugenio's digressions. After so many years, the Maldonada perversity still took him by surprise, forced him to admit the precariousness of custom. These people had not signed *any* social contract. But where Laura's unpredictability still had the power to quicken him, Eugenio's discordant drifting was making him frantic to escape from the room. But he had begun to speak of his mother.

"You should have seen her when she was still a young woman. She let herself go so. Because there was a terrible weakness, you see, such a terrible weakness. . . . Of course, she was not *hard*. No . . . her *temperament* was soft. Romantic. That ghastly romanticism! And my brother, Carlos, *encouraged* her in it—both of them so unrealistic. She had that money, all that was left after my father died. After that war, the carpetbaggers came. And they took *advantage* of her. Everything had been burned to the ground except the great house, and she sold it for a mere *nothing*. And she came *here* when she could have gone back to Spain. Her parents offered her money to go home, to take us all back *there*." He looked up at Peter. "My God!" he cried out. Then he held up his jacket, tweaked the button he had sewed, then went to hang it next to the gray trousers.

"It was Carlos who persuaded her to buy the house on Long Island. He was only a boy—but he had such *influence* over her. The house was an evil sponge . . . it took all our money. There wasn't any more. And if it hadn't been for La Señora Gonzaga—" He went back to his chair and sat down stiffly.

"—if it hadn't been for that woman, we would have starved to death, in our house. My mother would not admit the *hardness* of the world. Do you know what she did? In the depression? She tried to sell fine embroidery. It was the only thing she knew how to do!" and he emitted a kind of piercing cry as though he could find no word for what he felt about his mother's folly.

"So she became Señora Gonzaga's *companion*. And received a recompense—a monthly amount, small but it kept us. But these last years, after La Señora died, after her son sold the plantation to some Americans, there was nothing. She was very *shrewd*, not at all like my mother. She kept her holdings until the second of her death, you see, through the war, after. . . . And now, there is Fidel Castro. And nothing of any of us left there in Cuba. You see, we made a terrible mistake. We thought it was *ignoble* to be shrewd, cunning. . . ."

"Well—it is, isn't it?"

"Oh—if you could have seen her when she was still *herself*. How *fastidious* she was, such a *lady*. I wonder if you understand what I mean? She still remembered the past then. When one forgets the past, there is nothing, is there?"

"I'm afraid I must go. I have to let Carlos know. It's quite late. I had better—"

"Do you know I was actually *thrown* out of people's homes? Led to the very door and asked to leave? You see, we weren't trained to do *anything*. When we began to go to school in this country, my mother was *amused*, as though it were all a whim. Mamá did not understand that one must be trained in *something* to survive. When I was eighteen or nineteen, I would go to stay with friends so I would get fed, have *shelter*. And I would stay and stay until they were forced to ask me to leave. And at home, Mamá and Carlos would talk endlessly of some new scheme—both of them sitting there, planning. About what? About nothing!"

"But Eugenio—Carlos was quite a good music critic. Not so long ago, I used to see his name everywhere. He must have learned—"

"No, no . . . you don't understand. Carlos *made it all up!* He read a few books. We *had* learned to read. And he was a very good mimic, you see, and his friends were musicians. We have all learned by imitation."

"That is how everyone learns at first," Peter said.

"Oh, yes, at first. But then they change. Somehow, they no longer imitate. They begin to *know*. But in my family, we could never do anything but imitate. We never *knew*."

He fell silent, so silent, so still that Peter leaned forward and strained to catch the sound of breathing as though Eugenio might be dying there in front of him. The dark, deep-set eyes were staring at him but he saw no recognition. Then, slowly, a saturnine smile touched Eugenio's lips.

"I don't think you understood me when I said I'd been *thrown* out of houses, did you?"

He could not answer; he had not understood. But he had heard the horror in Eugenio's voice, the horror of an unexpungeable memory.

"Perhaps you can imagine—not knowing what to do next. I mean, with one's entire life. I don't believe I ever had the pleasant experience of thinking small decisions were unimportant. What I mean is, living as though one

were suspended over a pit, that if one looked too eagerly in
the direction of the dining room, one could be dropped instantly into that pit. So every second of life falls into peril—
or safety. Peril or safety—has one picked up the correct
fork? Should one ask for another serving? Is one's coat
hanging in the place reserved for the master of the house?
Is the argument in the bedroom between one's friend and
his mother about one's continuing, exasperating, *unbearable* presence? I didn't know how to look for work. Can you
imagine that? Why, once I walked into a Brooklyn clothing
store looking for a clerk's job. I was struck dumb! I could
not speak: Do you know that now, for the first time in my
life, I have a savings account? Would you like to see my
little book?" He stood up and walked over to the suitcase
where he picked up the manila folder and began to untie
the string that bound it.

"Please," Peter said. "I do see how awful it has all been.
But I must go, let the others—" and stopped, hearing *others*. But there was only Carlos.

"Tell me, Eugenio," he said, trying to speak neutrally.
"Your sister insisted that Clara not be told of your mother's
death. I don't understand what to—"

"Here it is," Eugenio said, holding the blue passbook in
his hand. "It is *grotesque,* isn't it? That a person of my
age—but it isn't a large amount. Still, I've not had *any*
amount until recently. Do you think the banks are safe?"

"About Clara—"

"Clara? She's rather flighty, isn't she? I haven't seen her
in some time. I suppose you know that my mother took
care of her? Señora Gonzaga permitted my mother to take
Clara with her to Cuba when she accompanied the Señora

there. As you must have gathered, my mother was never insistent, but there was an exception. Clara. She did insist on taking Clara."

"I thought that Laura was simply distraught tonight— that she hadn't meant it, about Clara," Peter said.

"Meant it?"

"Clara is not to be told, she is not to come to the funeral."

"I know nothing about these things between Clara and my sister," Eugenio said impassively. He replaced his passbook in the envelope. "All these women in the family have some trouble, Laura, Mamá, Clara, with men."

"I wasn't speaking of men."

"When my mother came to this country, a very *respectable,* very rich man wanted to marry her, even with the children—but Carlos wouldn't *permit* it. He had frightful tantrums. I suppose you wouldn't suspect that about my brother. And, of course, my mother always gave in. She gave in to everything. I realized she was losing her hold on things when she began to neglect her hair. Her dresses were often so *soiled.* But when she was still in command of herself—"

Peter stood up. "I must go," he said. He had determined to take a taxi to Carlos. His bones ached. He was exhausted.

"She even sold her jewelry for nothing. There was quite a bit of it. She might as well have given it away. She gave everything away. I tried to introduce her to certain people—well-bred, very *refined* people who would have appreciated her, understood what she came from. But it was *impossible.* She was too far gone. She had no *discipline.*"

Then, he cried out in an anguished voice. "And she grew so old!"

Peter began to walk toward the office.

"Oh, I must thank you," Eugenio said with a strange truckling bow. "I do appreciate your coming here at such a late hour."

On a leaf from his note pad, Peter wrote down the telephone of the Clappers' hotel. "Here is Laura's number," he said, holding it out to Eugenio. "If you'll call in the morning . . ."

"Yes. Do you think it's too late to call now? I suppose it is. But—is there anything else? Anything more you know about my mother's death? Do you think she was alone when she died?"

"I wish I could tell you more. But I've told you all I know."

"If you could have *seen* her in the time before . . ." He stood, several feet away from Peter, staring at the room he lived in, his glance falling on the couch, the lamp, his clothes, the barred window. Peter sensed he must often stand like that, looking at the emblems of his survival, measuring the scant space he had scraped out for himself.

"I'm sorry to have brought you such news," Peter said, walking quickly to the door that led to the street. He was full of a nervous apprehension that Eugenio might not let him out, but Eugenio slipped past him and unbolted the door.

"Well," he said, "if you ever plan a trip, I'm quite good at all that. You might be surprised at how good I am."

He promises surprises, he still waits to be thrown out, thought Peter as he stood shivering on the curb, looking up the avenue for a taxi. When, shortly, one came, it swerved recklessly toward him, its wheels sending up a spray of water from the gutter that soaked his trousers and socks. Inside the car, a becapped and neckless driver began at once to emit a demented croak of "Where to? Where to? Where to?" Peter gave Carlos's address in an icy voice and folded himself damply against the back seat. The driver shouted. "I just heard on the news about them dragging this woman out of the East River where she jumped. Let them die, I say. They want to kill themselves, let them!"

"I would rather not talk," Peter declared. He saw a patch of livid skin, a large wart, a gray patch of hair as the driver glanced back at him. In Peter's inner vision, the squad formed, raised its guns, fired. The cabdriver became an ash, blew away. These executions in his mind were taking place with increasing regularity; could one stink, spiritually, of a slaughterhouse, Peter wondered? Then, as they neared the east 60's, the driver erupted, "You know how to take care of this colored crime? You line them up, a dozen every day, then you shoot them. That's how." He drew to the curb and shut off his meter. "Know what I mean?"

"Why only a dozen?" Peter said as he handed him the fare. "Why not thousands?" and slammed the door.

In the entrance of the old apartment house where Carlos lived, he pressed Carlos's bell. When there was no response, he held his thumb on the button in a rage of shot nerves, his flesh chilled, his nostrils filled with the stale smell of dust and old metal polish. A sepulchral voice spoke through a grid at the side of the mailboxes.

"Who is it?"

"Peter Rice," he shouted into the grid, and grabbed the

doorknob as an electric buzzer sounded. There was no doorman here, only a dirty mirror near the elevator in which he caught a glimpse of his bedraggled self as he went to the stairs. Above him, from the second-floor landing, Carlos looked down.

"Peter! For God's sake! What brings you here at such an hour?" He was smiling, holding out his hand. Peter shook it, dropped it.

"I have to see you—"

"Come in, come in . . . listen, I've got a young friend here—a young chap . . ."

The doorway led directly into a kitchenette. A fluorescent light coated a sinkful of dirty dishes yellow. On the counter was half of a squeezed lemon.

Carlos was trying to take his coat but Peter wrapped himself in it stubbornly. For a moment there was savage confusion, hands flying, hands gripping, and suddenly Peter tore himself away into the living room and stood with his back against the wall as though at bay. A tall thin figure moved idly away from the windows which looked out on the street.

"This is Lance," Carlos said in a bewildered voice as a handsome, young dark-brown man sauntered to a couch and fell softly among its cushions. "Lance, this is an old friend, Peter Rice." The young man nodded, unsmiling, indifferent.

On the floor, near a fireplace, was a still life—two pillows, an empty glass, an ashtray overflowing with cigarette butts—from which Peter averted his eyes quickly.

"I'm just staying for a minute," he said, vaguely aware he owed some explanation for holding onto his wet raincoat which Carlos was still looking at curiously. Peter looked directly at Carlos, then at the young man, who now appeared to be dozing. A heavy chain circled his throat; suspended from it, visible upon his chest revealed by his open shirt, was a stone-encrusted pendant, vaguely Oriental.

"Well, yes, by all means, Peter. Would you like a drink. Do sit down. Won't you let me take the coat? You look like a rain forest. Don't worry about Lance. Just go ahead," Carlos nodded reassuringly.

"Laura sent me. They didn't want to telephone you about . . ."

Carlos's mouth tightened. He looked frightened.

"What is it," he said in a low voice.

"Your mother died."

Carlos looked straight up at the ceiling, then burst into clamorous violent sobs. His mouth fell open, enormous tears flowed down his chin, his hands thrashed the air. Lance flew to him and threw his arms around Carlos's massive shoulders. "Poor old thing . . ." he murmured. "Poor old thing has lost its Mama. . . ." He stroked Carlos's bald head, his neck, his wet face, and Carlos bent his head until it rested on Lance's narrow shoulder.

"Oh, God! Oh God!" he cried out.

"I'm sorry. I'm so—"

Carlos gasped, one of his hands reached out and seemed to clutch at the air. "Oh, tell me—" he began, then fell into another fit of weeping.

"Hush, hush, darling man," said Lance, and led him to the couch where he lowered him, his long back straining with the effort to support Carlos's weight. He fell beside him, endlessly stroked him. "Oh, what tears!" he said softly.

Peter retreated into the kitchenette where he leaned

back against the sink. He didn't think that, at this moment, he could stand upright without support. He was being persecuted by the sounds of lamentation in the other room; those explosive heated sobs seemed operatic and profligate, as though Carlos was desperately simulating grief in order to ward it off. But what had he expected? Indifference? Irony? Ritual gravity? He had not foreseen his own helplessness, this sudden, shocking intimacy, even though purely circumstantial, with the Maldonada brothers, his entrapment in the toils of a real, infinitely complex history which had been, up until tonight, all story, Laura's narration, to which he had wanted to be no more than a listener.

What a foul, neglected stench there was in this place! He plucked the lemon from the counter and held it to his nostrils. There was silence from the living room. At any moment now, he would be able to leave. Then he thought of Clara. His heart sank; something held off for so long had stepped up to him and was breathing on his cheek. Laura's narration had come to an abrupt stop in a tangle of raveled ends, in a heap of collapsed scenery. He felt he had been stripped naked, and he was strange to himself. As he stood away from the sink, a faint shudder passed through him.

"Please, Peter. Come in and sit down," Carlos called humbly from the other room.

He looked dazed, but his tears had stopped. Lance held one of his hands tightly. Peter sat down in a chair across from the couch.

"When did she die?"

"I think—I know it was this afternoon."

Carlos started. "But they only just found out about it?"

"Laura knew. She had heard this afternoon."

"I can't stand it!" cried Carlos, snatching his hand away from Lance and clapping it to his forehead. "How could she—but I thought she was crazier than usual tonight. God! How could she be such an unholy bitch!"

"After you left, she got up and ran out. I don't know why. Clara was telling her about some animals. I suppose she was very upset all along," Peter said wearily.

"So, she knew all the time. She sat there, knowing. I'm finished with her. Finished!"

"You'll have to call them in the morning at the hotel. I don't know about the arrangements for the burial."

"What about my brother, Eugenio?"

"I've just come from him."

Carlos threw him a look of wry comprehension. "He was—as usual?"

"I don't know him that well."

"There is nothing to know. Lance, will you fix me some vodka and tonic? And if there's a lemon . . ."

"I think we used your last lemon," Lance replied in a light, drawling voice. "Can I fix you something?" he asked politely of Peter.

"Thanks, no. Nothing."

"I don't suppose you know how—"

"Only what I've told you."

"But can you imagine her knowing all the time?" He shook his head. "Do you understand such a thing? Of course, she's incapable of explaining herself, ever. I suppose you know that about Laura. You've known her long enough. But have you ever heard—"

"Carlos. She told me Clara is not to be told of your mother's death. She said she wouldn't be interested."

"Is that what she said? *Interested?*"

"Just that."

Lance returned and handed Carlos a glass of vodka and tonic. "You're out of ice cubes," he said.

"Thank you, darling," Carlos said gently.

Lance smiled faintly and sat down beside him on the couch again.

"Carlos. Don't you think Clara should be told?"

Carlos looked worried. He took a swallow from his glass.

"I don't know," he said. "My mother was very fond of Clara. I wouldn't think—would you?—that Laura would try to protect Clara, spare her the funeral. I suppose she's angry at her, angry because Clara wouldn't go to the home to visit my mother. But Laura! For God's sake! They were away for *years*—she and Ed drifting around the world. She never even sent a postcard! Do you think Laura meant it? She says a good deal she doesn't mean."

"I think she meant it."

"Then—I don't know what to say."

"But what about you? Don't you want her to be there? At the funeral?"

"Well—you know, Desmond did take care of a good deal. I have to admit that. I suppose they have a right—it hardly makes any difference to my mother, after all, whether Clara is there or not."

"Don't be obtuse," Peter said sharply. "You know funerals aren't for the dead!"

"We are born again," Lance said reverently. "Death is only a door."

"I don't think that's quite fair," Carlos said. "I don't think I'm obtuse at all—but these ceremonies—"

"Carlos!" Peter said urgently. "I've asked you what you thought. If you think she should be there."

"I don't think much of *should*," Carlos said evasively.

"Then, I'm not to tell her? You won't tell her?"

"But, that's what I meant—about Desmond and my sister. They've taken care of things to a large extent. I suppose it's up to them, isn't it? How things are to be done?"

"You have no opinion?"

"No one wants to go to funerals, surely!"

"Is it a matter of desire?"

"I don't know what you're getting at. Really."

"But Clara is her only grandchild!"

"I know that! God knows, she could get none from Eugenio or me!"

"I think I'd better go."

"It was immensely good of you to come and tell me. I imagine they woke you up? I don't see why they couldn't have telephoned me in the morning." He paused, then went on. "I'll tell Ed. He'd want to know. They got along, you know. It was strange to see them together. She thought him a marvel. He was at his best with her. His best was very, very good. He really paid attention to her. He could imitate her wonderfully." He looked broodingly at Peter. "But you know all that, don't you? You know all about us."

"I don't know about Clara," Peter said. "I really don't know what to do. I think she ought to be there tomorrow, Carlos, won't you call her?"

Carlos stood up and began to pace about the room. Lance watched him, leaning forward as though ready to rush to him if he showed signs of collapse.

"Don't you think you're making a great deal out of little, Peter?" asked Carlos. He stood next to a large old upright piano, raising and lowering the keyboard lid. "Anyway, if Clara knew Laura didn't want her there, she certainly

wouldn't go. She's afraid of her, which isn't surprising.
Aren't we all?" Carlos smiled faintly. Then he said, "I can't
tell her at any rate. It's not my decision. It won't be a real
funeral. We have to put my poor mother in the ground,
that's all.

"Wasn't she a Catholic?" asked Peter.

Carlos laughed aloud. "Mamá? Of course she was Catholic. All Spaniards are Catholics." He banged down the
piano lid suddenly. "Did Laura ever tell you about my
grandfather? He was a philosopher of sorts. He wrote a
book, an anticlerical tract, and had a hell of a time back
then with the church. He hated priests the way only Latin
Catholics can hate them. Mamá never went to mass. That
went, too, like the rest of it. The priests and nuns made
her laugh, she made fun of them. I don't remember, natu-
rally, but I'm sure we were baptized. Although not confirmed, I think. There was a chapel on the plantation, I've
been told. But my father died, and that was the end. Although, now that I think about it, she went to a synagogue
once, and to several Protestant services. She used to say
she liked to know about everything." There was a touch of
mockery in his voice. "*Me gusta saber de todo,*" he repeated in Spanish. "I teased her about the synagogue. I
told her she was returning to the bosom of Abraham. Perhaps, she said."

"I *love* it when you speak Spanish," said Lance.

Carlos suddenly covered his eyes with his hand. "What a
terrible life," he said wretchedly.

"Listen!" begged Peter. "I've known you most of my life.
I don't know what happened to Clara, really. I've not
thought about it. She was born, then she was someone I
hardly ever heard about. I haven't asked. But your mother

was made to be responsible for her. It seems utterly wrong to me that Clara should not know she's dead. How will she find out? In three months, if she happens to drop by to see you? When she meets up with Laura again? What will Laura say? 'By the way, my mother is dead'? One should learn of a death in a family. How will she learn of it, then? Carlos! For God's sake, don't hide out in your own *character*—don't exploit your vices to get out from under! I know all about that! I do it, I do it myself. Answer me! Tell me what to do! Don't leave me with this—this weight!"

"Laura told you what to do," Carlos shouted, stalking across the floor toward Peter, then turning abruptly into a shadowed corner of the room. "You like to do what Laura wants, don't you?" He grunted something to himself, then shook his head roughly like a bull tossing its horns. "You always have," he went on rancorously. "How well I remember that first day, years ago, that you met them—in that house they had out on the island. But, do you remember? She had no love-sick suitor as faithful as you. All these years, you've been that, haven't you!"

"It's not important what I've been!" cried Peter.

"The bride of your heart," Carlos jeered. "Even Ed gave her up years ago, *years* ago! But you! I've seen you cringe when she raised her hand, and when she held it out, I've seen you lick it. And you ask *me* what to do about Clara? I don't know what to do about myself, about my brother, about Laura—and my mother. I've turned and turned away and always they were there, waiting, Laura crouched to spring out at me, my mother always waiting for me, that God-awful brave smile, waiting for me as though I was the hope of everything, of change, of possibility. What possibility? What could I have done for Eugenio? For any of them? We were wrecked from the beginning!"

"It's Karma," Lance remarked.

"Poor Clara," Carlos said in an exhausted voice. "She was the last one I could have done something for. But she has her life before her—she's well out of it. Tell her not to look back, not to join us wives of Lot. After all," he said with a sad smile, "she's an American girl. An enviable creature to be. Do you understand? I don't care whether she goes to my mother's funeral or not. It makes no difference at all."

Peter stood up. In the silence, Carlos stared at him without expression, his arms hanging loose at his side. Peter waited. Carlos walked forward out of the shadows. "As I said, I'm grateful to you. It's a thankless task you've had. But I thank you."

"I'll go then."

"I'll phone them in the morning. Perhaps we can have lunch one of these days? Perhaps you'd like to see Ed? He's not always entirely drunk. If you could come up here from your office—Ed is frightened by that midtown crowd. There's a quiet Italian restaurant not far from here. I'm sure Ed would like to see you."

Peter nodded. At the door, as he opened it, Carlos said, "Be sure to remember me to your sisters when you see them."

At the foot of the stairs, Peter sat down. He heard the door click closed. It was nearly 3:00 A.M. He thought of Gina sitting on those other stairs. He felt singularly alone. His sisters were close as a married couple, smiling at him from the fastness of their devotion to each other, excluding him as they always had excluded him. But if he died, now, here on the stairs, this pain in his left arm the first tremor of a collapsing heart, his sisters would see that he had a proper funeral. And for a second, recalling their voices from another room, their feet pounding through the old house as they went out to play, leaving him behind, he thought, how could I be so old? How could they have lived so long? Is that all there is? This withering and softening and exhaustion in time?

It was dangerously late to be out on the streets. He had often boasted of his fears. Like everyone he knew, he was inclined to brag about fear. Another dodge. Perhaps Laura had said nothing about the death, had kept silent in order to postpone the news to herself. Wasn't that it? Ed Hansen had told him a story once of a man who, after he had been hit by a train at a crossing, had walked a mile before he fell, every bone in his body broken.

All these years Carlos and he had floated along the currents set into motion by a youthful and unquestioning friendship. Yet all the time, Carlos had been judging him, observing him, drawing up accounts. But how wrong he was! Peter had never suffered the sickness of love for Laura. It was something else.

On Lexington Avenue, he found a telephone booth, but there was no directory. After two phone calls to information, he was able to elicit Clara's address by giving the operator one he made up. It was twelve blocks away. He began to walk uptown on Lexington. He was not thinking of what he would do. He was recalling how exposed he had been in the telephone booth, and how he had not been frightened. Let them kill him! But no sooner had he given permission to unknown assailants, then he was engulfed by horrible apprehensions. It was as though, all at once, his nerves had been hooked up to some galvanic pulse of malign energy. He trembled; in the pockets of his raincoat, his clenched hands sweated; his eyelids twitched. He was shambling toward disintegration, in a state of fear so elemental that his mind, streaming always with words, became a screen over which light and dark had ceased to play.

Some purely physical reflex brought him to a halt against a shop window against whose cold glass he leaned his forehead. He was panting like a dog. Gradually, his vision returned. He saw, in the window, bathed in the glow of a small spotlight, a model ship. It was a schooner in full sail. On the deck, tiny figures of sailors bent at their tasks. One was on the aft rigging; the rigging itself was of flax-colored rope, intricate, taut, perfect, a thing he could have examined forever, this work of skill and patience, an imitation of reality that was in itself a realization. His breathing grew normal. The blurred symbols in his head took shape, became orders. He would tell Clara that her grandmother had died that day. He did not know what else he would tell her. He'd see. He went on. A couple in evening clothes approached, then passed him. He saw pinned to the woman's fur coat a large white button upon which black letters read: "Fuck Housework."

He thought of other proclamations, other times. He lived in a period of disgust, of self-disgust, of disgust with all others, of a sickly, puerile, sentimental detestation of thought which led without divagation to the cabdriver's solution of crime and to his own silent firing squad.

He was very cold. The drizzle of rain continued. He had had what Violet would have called, and instantly dismissed as, an attack of anxiety. But that supernal dread which had caught him up with such violence could not be encompassed by the propitiating lingo of psychology. Naming had scant magic when magic itself was at work. Yet as he sloshed, exhausted, toward Clara's apartment, he felt a touch of felicity, as though the resolution that was leading him toward her was about something other than death.

CHAPTER SIX

Clara

"Yes, it is nice. I pay more rent that I can really afford. But when I saw this big room—I thought, if I have such a room, I won't mind anything else. There's a joke kitchen over there. The bedroom is only large enough for a bed. And this street isn't bad. Did you notice the little house next door? It's supposed to be a Stanford White house. Was the doorman unpleasant to you? He was a star reporter on a newspaper, then it folded, and he was too old to get what he calls decent work. He was quite mean when I moved in, sneering at how little furniture I brought. But it was just to get me interested in him so he could tell me he wasn't an ordinary doorman, that he'd been important once. I couldn't think who it was when the buzzer rang. Let me take your coat. Is it still raining hard?"

"I've been out for a while," Peter said, handing her the coat. There was only one small closet in the place, she told him, so she would hang it in the bathroom.

The room was plain, clean, and spacious. It was sparsely furnished, a studio bed covered with sailcloth, three cane chairs, two small tables, one long table covered with a brilliant green oilcloth. He picked up a small volume that lay on the couch. *The Spirit of the Age* by William Hazlitt. There were no other books, no magazines. On one wall hung two drawings side by side. One was signed, Edward Hansen. It showed a cluster of flat-roofed houses on a curve of beach. The other was an unsigned sketch of a leafless tree, thickly branched, with a twisted trunk like that of an olive tree.

"That's a place where they lived a while," Clara said when she returned to the living room and found him looking at the drawings. "I think it was Italy."

"The tree is very nice."

"I did that."

"You didn't sign it."

"No."

"Do you draw a lot?"

"Not at all. I did that one night from memory. It was the only tree that looked like that on the plantation in Cuba where I lived with my grandmother. All the other trees looked like giraffes or hedgehogs. Actually, it had leaves, but I couldn't remember how they were shaped."

"You ought to do more. I always wanted to draw."

"No. I don't really care about drawing," she said, sitting down in one of the chairs. "It was just a personal thing."

She had changed from her dress into gray slacks and a gray sweater and she was wearing summer sandals on her bare feet. He noticed they were narrow and bony and, like the room, extremely clean. She was watching him intently, but he felt she was not aware of her own intentness, only that she was determined to show no surprise at his being there at such an hour.

"Do you like Hazlitt?" he asked, sitting down on the couch, wondering how long he was going to postpone an explanation of his presence. It was not only politeness, he thought, that was preventing her from questioning him. She looked braced, her calmness the result of will. Without makeup now, she seemed older than she had looked in the hotel room and the restaurant. He was abashed. Had all the anguished resolution which had brought him here been uncalled-for, self-serving? In her living presence, he realized he had been thinking of her as a child. She was regarding him gravely, sitting straight in the chair. She was pale, unadorned like her room. Her voice was different from what he remembered. How odd to think Laura could affect one's vocal chords. She had spoken hastily, softly, during dinner, as though on the run. He listened to her voice now; it was cool and somewhat hollow.

"Hazlitt is all right," she said. "I don't keep books. As long as there's a library nearby, I can get what I want. All my friends are weighted down with books, and when they have to move, they just curse them. But they keep on buying them."

"You don't read novels?"

She looked suddenly restive. He said, quickly, "I'm awfully glad I didn't wake you. I was afraid I would have to and it was a relief—"

"Listen, I got hungry and made myself some toast just before you came. Would you like a piece?" She was smiling uneasily. He felt he was tormenting her. Yet he couldn't say what he had to.

"No, no. But you go ahead. Don't let me—"

The smile disappeared. She merely looked at him, waiting.

"I don't know how to go about this," he said. Why didn't she help him? Couldn't she ask him why he'd come?

"You're scaring me a little."

"It's about your grandmother."

She glanced at Hansen's drawing, then back to Peter. Her hands flattened out on her thighs.

"Something happened," she said suddenly, her voice rising.

"She died this afternoon."

She stood up at once and walked to the long table where she stood with her back turned to him. She was thin, he thought, much too thin. She turned slowly until he could see her face. She was not crying. Her face seemed frozen. He thought, I mustn't show surprise if she laughs. Sometimes people do laugh when they learn of a death—I mustn't—

"My mother sent you to tell me?"

It was the question he had feared, pushing it back all along, claiming to himself he only needed to deliver the news of death. He heard her repeat it as she began to walk toward him, her hands clasped in front of her. He was terrified that she might kneel and beg him to answer. Now she stood directly in front of him. Hardly aware of what he was doing, he began to turn the pages of the Hazlitt. A folded piece of paper dropped from the book to his knee. Clara bent forward and picked it up delicately with two fingers and slipped it into the pocket of her slacks. Only a few seconds had passed.

"No," he said.

She fell into a chair.

"I don't understand," she said, her voice quavering.

"I mean—she said you were *not* to be told."

She flushed violently; redness streaked her pale skin like a rash. Her lips parted. He could see the gleam of a tooth. Then she glanced at various objects in the room, her head turning rapidly, her glance resting only a second on this thing or that. But she didn't look at him. She looked awkward, helpless, as though something heavy had fallen on her and was pinning her down. He didn't know what to do, how to explain, how to help her.

"I know how shocked you are," he said, just above a whisper, not wanting to recall her harshly to his presence there, to his witnessing what he realized was humiliation, not grief.

"I'm not shocked," she said. "She was so old and sad. What else was there for her to do in that awful place? And I would have expected Laura—" But she stopped speaking.

It was far more painful than he had imagined. Constrained to say something, he repeated her "expected" weakly as if offering her her own word so she could go on.

"I'm lying," she said. She drew up her legs and folded her arms across her breasts. "It's not what I expected at all. How could anyone—how *could* I have expected that Laura would not tell me? It's my way—not to show surprise."

She looked at him with an angry, nettled expression. "I don't give a damn either," she said, "but I suppose if Laura came here with a pistol and aimed it at my head, I'd ask her if she wanted a drink before she fired."

He said, "I don't know what Laura could have been thinking. It's certainly possible that she was too upset to know what she was saying."

"Laura always knows what she's doing and saying," Clara said vehemently. "She is not, as many people are, constrained by self-consciousness. She doesn't care *why* she does things. Have you ever known anyone else for whom cause and effect are the same thing? She has always been *charmed* by my efforts to justify her own actions to her."

She had spoken without emphasis, but ruthlessly, and he heard how much at this minute her voice did sound like her mother's.

"But she must have been distraught—the death of a parent—" he began.

"Never mind that!" she said harshly. "I know all that! But can't you tell me anything?"

"About Laura—" he began, but she was shaking her head from side to side, and he fell silent, watching her worriedly. He had thought he only wanted to do the right thing, that he was doing the right thing. But he hadn't taken her into account.

She leaned toward him. "Is it because I hardly ever went to see Alma? Is she getting even with me? Laura believes in revenge—if belief is the word for it. What I'm asking you is—explain, tell me!" she implored him. "Why am I not to know? Please. I don't want universal truths. That's no trouble. My grandmother died all alone. Would you have whispered in *her* ear that everyone dies? Listen to me!" She paused and looked down at her clenched hands. "It's the difference that's so hard—your own life is the difference."

"I know that," he said.

"How would you feel? If it were you? If you were shut out?"

"I don't know," he answered.

"No, you don't," she agreed.

"I can imagine," he said quickly.

"Why do I feel so ashamed?" she cried at him. "Why this awful shame? . . ."

"I'm sorry. I really am sorry. I hate Laura for this."

"Do you?" she asked. "Can you hate her?"

The room was cold. He shivered a little, then glanced at his watch. He hadn't gone without sleep like this for years. Clara was lighting a cigarette.

"I said I could imagine how you felt," he said. "Isn't there any comfort in that?"

"Is there?" she asked.

"She was jealous of you, maybe," he said. "Her mother took care of you. I got the impression you were the only person anyone ever took care of in that family."

"Jealousy? Is that it?"

"I don't know."

Clara looked calmer all at once, settled into trouble.

"Even if it is jealousy, what difference does it make?" she asked without interest. "Laura is a terrorist. She realizes herself only when the bomb she throws explodes. It's a self-realization I don't understand."

"Why do you see her?"

"I don't know how *not* to see her."

"But she doesn't try to see you, does she?"

"She has an impulse now and then."

"Don't go. You don't have to."

"If it were a question of will . . ."

"Can you make it that?"

"I haven't been able to yet. But after this, it might be easier."

"I've known your mother a long time," he said. "I know in my bones she was wretched tonight."

"I don't pretend that she didn't feel anything. But, Jesus! She's dead cold inside, half born. She doesn't really know that anyone else is alive. The world—it's only an expanded bubble of herself—what she hates is part of herself. The Jews, you know how she is about Jews? Yet those Hebrew ancestors aren't one of Ed's fancies. She never gets *outside* anything. Didn't you feel it tonight, in the restaurant, when she was teasing you about your work? And talking about Carlos's piggishness? How she sees everything as designed for her or against her?"

"I can see why you would feel that way," he said.

"How I'd feel that way!" she exclaimed. "I'm talking about you! Can't you say anything—something to me about what she's done? Don't you see? I don't even know if she's not right! But, goddamn her! It was me that lived with her mother. Oh, Christ! I'm sick with thinking about her. I was born thinking about her."

"And your grandmother?" he asked. "What about her?"

She didn't answer for a long time. She sat there, smoking, her eyes closed. Then she stubbed out her cigarette in an ashtray on the table next to the chair.

"I don't know about that either," she said at last. "I'm scared. But grief?" She looked at him steadily for a minute. "I hated her when I was a child," she went on. "I don't know why. She was never brutal to me. We were like two castaways in a lifeboat. The supplies were always on the point of giving out. I *felt* that. I never took daily life for granted. She was so subservient, yet she managed to force those two, my uncles, to come Sunday after Sunday for those horrible dinners. It was like a slaughter, one of those dinners, Carlos with his eyes rolled up like a martyr whose feet are on fire, Eugenio exuding poisonous rage while she pretended to laugh, pretended there was an actual living conversation going on. My grandmother ruled them, through the tyranny of her pathos. No one seemed able to stop anything, to change the way it was."

"You must have been pretty confused."

"No," she said emphatically. "The life with her was all I knew. It simply penetrated me. I didn't think about it."

"But she was very fond of you. I've always heard that."

"I bet you heard that," she said with a certain hardness.

"But wasn't she?" he insisted.

"Well, I suppose. But I hated the way she made me feel. She surrounded me like a fog. She would ask me to kiss her. I would brush my face against hers, my lips flattened, holding my breath. Once, I told her she smelled bad. She laughed a little wistful laugh. I knew how cruel I was being—and I felt a kind of pleasure in it, that cruelty. If she had slapped me—but I never saw her in a rage. At that point where I would expect her to be angry, her tears would start. And yet, we only had each other in that place where we lived. She came to parents' day once at the public school I went to. She walked like a cripple—her feet gave her such trouble and the pain must have thrown her off balance—but she was dressed so differently from the other parents, in her flowing rags, and her hair was coming undone all through the class period. I kept turning in my seat to see if it had come all the way undone. There was her accent, but you met her, didn't you? She had such a *willful* accent—like a comic stage-Latin. She kept smiling at me from the back of the classroom as though there was nothing strange about her being there, or about the two of us. I was embarrassed. In the center of my life, there was an awful embarrassment."

"Always?" he asked.

"You spoke of will," Clara said sadly. "When I grew up, I willed it away, my mortification. Oh—I knew it was wrong, *humanly* unjust. And I used to go to see her when she was still living in the apartment. I brought her presents. But I always felt dislike, a distance from her, and she wanted *everything* from me, not just presents. It was a weak little stream of obligation that took me there, and when she went to the home, it dried up altogether. She was like a locked room I had escaped from. And all the time, I felt ugly with ingratitude, knowing how I *should* have felt."

"What on earth did those two, Ed and Laura, do with you in the beginning?" he asked. But he was speaking in his "story" voice; he had drawled out the question the way he sometimes did in an editorial meeting with a writer whose inflamed self-esteem forced him into ludicrous circumspection.

She caught the tone and looked at him ironically.

"Why—I was born and instantly pressed into Alma's arms," she said.

"So, she took care of you. You can't get away from that," he said, willing her silently to say what he wanted her to say, that she would go to the funeral and justify his interference, release him from this obligation to listen any further to her.

"I know!" she burst out. "Oh, God! I *know* she took care of me. Who else was there?"

"You could have been sent away—to strangers."

"I found them less strange," she said.

"And she took you to Cuba—that couldn't have been easy for her from what I've heard. That was something, wasn't it?"

"What are you up to? What are you after?" she demanded.

"You're awfully easy on yourself. You don't know what could have happened—with strangers."

"I'm not claiming I know. I only know what did happen."

"I don't know so much about it, but I have the sense her life was a long disappointment. I saw Eugenio tonight. I had to stop by to tell him—"

"Eugenio!" she interrupted. "That lunatic!"

"He told me how your grandmother had tried to sell embroidery during the depression. It was always hard times for her. She was alone with those three. He told me some things about himself that he'd lived like a beggar, a sponge. . . ."

"Don't you see?" she importuned him. "I've heard it all. I *lived* it."

Angrily, he said, "You didn't live *her* life. You can't seem to acknowledge that she was there, sheltering you."

She ignored what he'd said and began to talk about Cuba. "I hardly ever saw her there, once or twice a month maybe. She was at the beck and call of that old witch, Gonzaga, who went absolutely out of her head the last year of her life. All for $200 a month. Everything came from Gonzaga—she'd even arranged my grandmother's marriage to Maldonada. Oh—how it comes back to me! When we left that squalid apartment, and got on the Myrtle Avenue line with our baggage, and an hour or so later, we boarded Gonzaga's private train that was hopping with servants like fleas. A private train! And the plantation like an industrialized feudal village, people bowing to the old woman. They put me in a room next to the servants' wing.

Night and day I could hear the bells that summoned them.
The smell of cane, such a dark, sulky smell, and miles of it
growing twenty feet high all around the village with its
shacks built on stilts, and underneath them pigs and
chickens cackling and grunting. There was such a smell
of tropical rot over everything but the servants scoured it
away from the great house, kept it at bay. But still, stray
dogs would run among the grapefruit trees, their ears full
of swollen ticks, like white grapes, even into Gonzaga's
private garden where a valet wheeled her on the afternoons she was not hallucinating. . . . The servants gave
me liquor-soaked rags to give to Gonzaga's monkeys—to
get them drunk. She had cages of monkeys and tropical
birds in the garden. And the servants let me visit them in
their little rooms. But they wouldn't touch me. And I had
another life no one in the great house knew about." She
smiled reminiscently. "I found my way out of the gardens.
I found the village schoolteacher, Maria Garçia was her
name . . . in the afternoons, she used to bathe me, along
with her own children, in a metal tub in her kitchen, then
put up my straight hair in brown paper twists so it would
curl, and afterwards, she would take us all for the *paseo*,
the afternoon walk. When I got back to the big house, no
one asked me where I'd been. I don't think they knew I'd
been anywhere."

"But there were good times then?" he asked.

She ignored the question. She said, "Gonzaga was rich
in the old way. The Gonzaga family had been very smart—
so many of those old families lost their estates after the
war with this country, but Gonzaga had dealt and compromised and held on and paid. One night a flock of guinea
fowl began to cry outside my window and I was scared and

ran into the corridor, toward the central part of the house.
I wasn't ever supposed to go there, but I didn't dare wake
any of the servants. And I ran straight into a group of
musicians, taking a break, I guess, outside the main salon.
Their backs were turned to me, and each one was holding
in his fingers a dark cheroot, the smoke rising up like a
screen. Gonzaga had summoned them from Havana. And
she had her own personal doctor who lived with her, and
her priest, and that private train, and a yacht that was
always kept ready for her though she was too feeble to ever
use it. You see? It was that kind of wealth."

"Your grandmother had no choice," he said. "She did
what she could."

"I'm not blaming anyone."

"Did you think everyone else had it better?"

"Once. I thought that once," she said caustically.

"It's done damage, this idea of happiness, what it is,
what one is owed."

"I suppose so," she said. "But I wish—" and she stopped
and seemed to wait for him to tell her what she wished.

"Perhaps you cared about your grandmother more than
you think," he said.

She laughed at him. "I wouldn't have thought you were
so simple-minded," she said.

"*You* are!" he retorted, stung.

"Now I've made you mad," she said. "But maybe you're
right. Maybe that is what I wished, that I *could* have cared
about her. But I didn't. It was Carlos I loved. He's sweet,
you know, really sweet. I think I used to dream he'd take
me away with him. I knew he wouldn't. I knew he never
could do much for anyone. But he was never bitter—like
the others. I suppose my grandmother was sweet, too,

when she was a girl, before it all began, that long voyage to Cuba, to the man she'd never met and had to marry. She was only sixteen, you know. He was thirty-eight. But, yes . . . I remember times when she was not servile and plaintive, when she was amused, when something made her laugh. She was a good mimic. She used to imitate Eugenio perfectly. It takes a certain hardheartedness to be a good mimic. When she was like that, I felt a weight had been lifted from our life together. But there was another side to her, a morbid side. She used to tell me ghastly stories, people depositing severed hands in someone's bed, stories of curses that brought disease and death. Cuban voodoo."

Peter felt drained of strength, without conviction that he should be where he was. He said, "I haven't been up this late for a decade."

"I'll ring downstairs and get the old star reporter to find you a taxi," she said. "I've kept you too long."

"You didn't keep me," he said. "But wait—wait just a minute."

She watched him guardedly. He thought, I can go now, but he said, "I think you must go to her funeral."

"No!" she cried. "Not a chance!"

"You're going to let Laura have her way?"

"I don't care about Laura's way. I won't go. And don't tell me what funerals are for. I know all about that. This is different."

"It's not different," he said. "It's a death, your grand-mother's. You have no right to stay away."

"Rights have nothing to do with it. I don't believe in such rights. And who gave you the right to tell me what to do?"

"No one. And I'm asking you, not telling you."

"I have something to do tomorrow—today. It is almost day. And it's important to me."

She looked composed, cold. She'd walked away from the trouble. He disliked her suddenly; he was chilled by her callousness. Let her play dead then! There was nothing for him to do—it wasn't his affair. Laura would telephone him in a few days. It would be as it always had been. He had pressed up against enough Maldonada thorns. Eugenio alone would have been enough!

Clara was silent. He had a sudden vision of himself raising his foot and bringing it down on her bare feet. She had a hard nature. She was arranging her face to show indifference.

"What's so important to you?" he asked, his voice cracking with anger.

She wrenched herself upright. She looked astonished.

"And don't tell me it's none of my business," he said. "Are you going to let it go on forever, this thing with Laura. Are you going to let her be the one who decides forever? End it! Go for yourself!"

"I wouldn't go to *her* funeral either," she said stupidly. She looked down at her lap, her eyes half closed.

He slumped against the wall behind the couch. He wanted to go home, to sleep, to rejoin his silent life, to know where everything was.

"I'll tell you what it is," she said hesitantly.

"I don't care."

"There is a day planned—with a man. We haven't ever had a chance for a whole day together until now. It might not come again."

"Whose man?"

She laughed scornfully. "For God's sake! Not that! Are you going to tell me—"

"I'm not going to tell you anything," he replied. "It was a conclusion, an observation, whatever you like. It's not much of a reason anyhow."

"I guess not," she admitted. She looked at him candidly. "I liked the idea, that he had to plan for it, be quick to see a chance, fix it all up, just to spend a few hours with me."

"And you?"

"I feel his pleasure."

"Is that all?"

"Isn't it enough?"

"I don't know."

"But how *can* I go if she doesn't want me there?"

"By finding out where the burial is to take place—by finding out how to get there—by dressing yourself and going."

"I can't do it," she said and stood up and began walking around the room. "It's chilly, isn't it? They stop sending up enough heat at this time of the year. It's nearly spring, isn't it?" She paused near a window and peered through it. "There's nobody on the street. It isn't often empty."

"I'll take you," he said. His heart sank, yet he'd known all along he'd make the offer. "I have a car. I can find out in the morning where she's to be buried, and get the car out of the garage, and drive you."

"I don't give a damn that she's dead!" she said, turning to him. "I simply don't give one damn!"

"Neither do I," he said. "But if I take you, will you go?"

"Go yourself!" she snapped. Then, smiling maliciously, she said, "Think how that would please Laura! That's what you like to do, isn't it? Bird calls and nasty stories, anything to please her?"

He was chagrined, yet he wanted to laugh. The impulse to laugh was powerful, like an incipient sneeze. Carlos, and now Clara, sniggering about his servitude. They were simply rattling their own chains. He started laughing. For no reason he could think of, he had suddenly recalled how his sister, Kitty—almost nineteen she must have been then—had picked up a tray holding his mother's prize tea set and hurled it to the floor, breaking every single piece.

"What's so funny?" he heard Clara ask through his laughter, then, her voice concerned, "Listen, are you all right?"

"I'm fine," he gasped. "Something I remembered. . . . I didn't laugh when it happened, but—it was something my sister once did. She smashed up a load of Spode one morning. It was the only time I remember Kitty going out of control like that. My mother kept a tea set on a tray in the dining room. For people to admire. We never used the stuff. The sideboard was wobbly and we always had to tiptoe in the dining room. 'Watch out for my Spode!' my mother would shout if she heard one of us in there. But she wouldn't move it to another place. She used to stare at it a good deal—" He broke off and began to laugh again. Clara's uncomprehending face provoked him to louder laughter. "I mean," he said, coughing, "I mean, my mother looked at it so *stubbornly*." He cleared his throat, snickered faintly. "I must have thought then that we'd been hit by an earthquake—everything would have to change. Nothing changed. And now, it seems funny."

"I'm sorry. I shouldn't have said that . . . about your pleasing Laura."

Another wave of laughter seized him. They both tried to ignore it as though he were belching uncontrollably. Then he said, "It's true, what you said. Say it. Say anything you

like. But it doesn't matter *how* Alma took care of you. She
did."

"You can't know what it was like for me," she said.

"I can guess," he said. "There's no end of trouble. My
mother was a good manager. She saw to us. But she was a
well-poisoner. She worked an awful magic between the
three of us children. Even when we were small, she would
report to us what the other two were saying. It was a kind
of careless whispering; it filled the house; she seemed to
feed on the gossip of her children. At night, when she'd
come to tuck me in, she'd say, 'Martha says you're being
very silly in your civics class—your little farm friend, Rob-
ert, told her so. Don't you think you'd better stop all that?'
and when I was older, 'Kitty tells me you had some friends
in when I was in Trenton yesterday and that you all sat
around being oh so important, talking about poetry! Well—
so you waited till your old peasant mother was out!' And
she always understood why a boy had cracked me over the
head, or a teacher found me unresponsive. She understood
everyone except herself. And even then, I knew there was
no intelligence at work, and no feeling except vindictiveness toward me because I was *hers*. Not that she didn't
do the same thing to my sisters. But there was some soli-
darity between them, an element that kept me out. When I
walked into a room where the three of them had been talking together, they went quiet, and I would feel awkward
and large, too large to retreat back through the door. Yet
she couldn't even criticize me without covering up. 'You
and I are so self-destructive, Petey,' she'd say. Of course, I
knew she only meant me. When Kitty married, the year
before Mother died, I used to hear her—'You can't expect
anything of men—don't be surprised if he's not there

when you really need him—men never are.' The marriage
didn't last long—although that wasn't entirely my mother's
fault. And sometimes, not often, when I rebelled, got mad
because of some tangled thing she'd said, she'd run to the
girls, in front of me, crying, 'Oh, look! I've hurt his feelings. He's so abnormally sensitive! I feel so guilty!' When
she died—" He hesitated. Clara was leaning forward in her
chair, staring at him intently. "When she did die, I was
glad, the way you are when a pain stops. But I was crazed
too, for a while."

"You didn't love her?"

"Love!" he exclaimed. "There's more to love than love."

"What else is there?"

"Well," he said, "there's thought."

"And your father?"

"David Clarey Rice," he said as though calling out his
own name. "My father. 'Our depressed paterfamilias,' my
mother called him. That uncle I was telling you about, the
one I made the pie with, he was my father's brother, rather
plain like him, a plain person, not dull, but unadorned by
temperament. My father never said much about himself.
In time, I think I've slowly comprehended them both, from
my own life. I see now how frantic she must have been.
And he was disappointed. He didn't have the language for
his disappointment, didn't know how to tell it. He was
kindly but toneless, as though he'd been swept clean of
even ordinary things—like irritability. He was like a shelter
where you could get in out of a storm. A silent place."

"You were angry a lot?"

"No. I wasn't. There was affection . . . something like it
anyhow."

"But you got out of it alive!" she said, evidently thinking

her own thoughts about herself. "It isn't much in your life anymore."

"You never get out of it."

"I have this trouble," she said with a certain humbleness. "I don't see things in a plain way. I can't be plain."

He laughed. "*You* have this trouble. . . ."

"I don't know what you're really up to," she said indignantly. "It's not just a matter of this—this mess not being your business. You stumble in here in the middle of the night sweating righteousness from every pore—and you don't seem to have the faintest thought of what you're stamping on and bruising. Do you think I'm going to do what you tell me to do? What anyone tells me to do?"

"Except Laura . . ."

"Not Laura!" she exclaimed furiously. "I arrived when everything was over—a consequence of Ed Hansen's momentary insistence. The Maldonadas should have died out—without issue. The three of them are like dinosaurs sinking into the tar pits, flailing about themselves—"

"When they were young—" he tried to interrupt.

"Ah, yes! And they were so different then? They weren't! They were merely young—"

"You're so stupid!" he cried. "You won't have to break your neck the way I did—you won't have to find out, too late, that nothing's been arranged for you!"

She smiled as though she'd caught him out.

"What about you?" she asked triumphantly. "What's between you and Laura? Why are you *pushing* me? What is it you want me to do for *you*? You could have left them to their own dead. If it was such an affront to your sense of propriety, you could have refused when she told you not to tell me. You coward!" Her voice had risen; she was hurling words at him like stones.

"I want you—" he began, holding up his hands as though to shield his face—"I want you to *break* it, break the fatality, stand at that grave!"

"For me?" she cried. "For my good? For yours! Isn't that it?"

"Yes. For all that!"

"You idiot!"

"All right!"

"It's all between you and that *outlaw!* It has nothing to do with me!"

"Yes," he said, defeated. "Maybe it is between Laura and me. She *is* outside the law. It's why I've loved her, hung on to her all these years."

"Then you go! Leave me out of it!" she demanded.

"No. I can't," he said. "It's because of you I'm here." He felt stupefied. His jaws ached. He said, barely audibly, "You must go and jump past her."

"Lay your own spooks," she said.

He pushed the Hazlitt essays to the floor and lay down full length on the couch and closed his eyes. He said, "Don't go. Wait for somebody to convince you of something, anything. That's what you expect to happen, don't you? After all, you're an American girl. . . . Don't go. I don't give a damn, just like you. I'm too exhausted to look at you, to look at your blank face. You can shove it!" He opened his eyes. The room was empty.

He felt fatigue as a blessing. He knew he couldn't stand up, and he was grateful to know it. He needed only to turn his head, away from the light to the wall, and he would fall asleep. Then he heard the chink of china.

"Here," Clara said. She was holding a tray in one hand. On it was a cup of tea, a slice of lemon, some sugar cubes, toast. She drew a small table close to the couch. "It's ice-cold, like English toast," she said.

She left the room and soon returned carrying a blanket and a pillow.

"It's a good couch for sleeping," she said.

"Do you really like to read Hazlitt?" he asked.

"Not very much. But it makes me feel calm; boredom makes me calm."

"The tea is a comfort, just as they say."

"I've set the alarm for eight o'clock," she said. "We'll get a few hours sleep, if we're lucky. You can call them then, at the hotel. Will you tell her then? That you've told me?"

"No," he said. "There's no point . . . you'll just be there."

She spread the blanket over him, then waited till he had put the cup down to slip the pillow beneath his head.

"Shall I take your glasses off?" she asked.

He loved the weight of the blanket. "I think I'll kiss this blanket," he said. She removed his glasses gently and put them on the table.

"You will go with me?" she asked.

"Yes," he said, his eyes closing.

CHAPTER SEVEN

The Funeral

Violet, holding a feather duster in one hand, was bending to the baseboard on the landing of the second floor as Peter climbed the stairs. She swung her body up and toward him until she was standing still, the duster held upright like a bouquet. He paused. Their eyes met. Her expression was one of complacent charity; she had taken a candid shot of him and she was sure of its truth. He had been out—astonishingly—with a woman. But he saw a trace of struggle in her smile. He guessed she had been listening, half consciously, for the sounds of his morning presence above her and had not heard them. Anger was not among the emotions she permitted herself. He stood there, seeing the very core of their connection, revealed like the core of a halved apple. Violet, kind, smug, jealous; he, recognizing the jealousy, faintly gratified by it, knowing she would deny to the death that she felt it. Upon her raft of toothpicks Violet sat, proclaiming that the boundless waste upon which she floated was no more than an inlet.

"Ah-ha!" she said brightly, "so there you are!" But he saw at once that she regretted her words. Hastily, she asked, "Is the rain still so heavy? Roger absolutely refused to wear his raincoat to school this morning. Ah—these children! I suppose they must rebel."

"Good morning, Violet. It's raining, but the wind has come up. It might blow over later today."

"You look like you could use a good cup of coffee," she suggested.

"I could, but I can't," he said.

She plucked distractedly at the feathers of the duster. He could see how much she wanted to ask him where he'd been, yet she felt she had no right. She settled for a kind of sporty motherliness.

"You look rather seedy," she said. "Are you feeling all right?"

"I'm tired. I've been up most of the night. I have to go to a funeral today."

"Oh, dear! Not someone close to you, I hope?"

"No. Only someone I knew. An old lady."

"Ah, well, then. It's a natural thing."

She was palpably relieved. "I'll tell you all about it later," he said. "I'll drop by."

She stood discreetly aside. He continued up to his floor, wondering if Gina was home frightening her mother with her morose presence. He couldn't remember if it was a day she went to her university classes.

Clara, her eyes ringed with fatigue, had made him breakfast. Then he had called the hotel. Desmond had answered, saying he had not yet reached the home but intended to call around nine. Peter was thankful for Desmond's characteristic lack of curiosity. He did not have to produce the excuse that he was calling in order to send flowers to the cemetery. He told Desmond he had seen both the brothers. Desmond did not inquire how they had

taken the news. How was Laura? Peter asked. Desmond
said she was taking a bath and had had some sleep. She
was fine, he said, considering.

Clara had listened, standing around edgily, drinking her
coffee as though on the run. He had asked her if she
wouldn't have to phone her office. "You forget," she had
said. "I've already taken care of that."

"Do you want me to go?" he asked. "I can telephone you
later as soon as I find out."

"If you don't mind," she had replied. "It's only that my
friend is coming here to pick me up at nine." She smiled at
him suddenly with a certain delicacy. "Then I'd have to
explain your being here."

His avuncular laugh sounded utterly false to him, but he
said, "Thank you for even thinking of it."

He let himself into his apartment. The plant seemed to
have dropped another hatful of leaves while he'd been out.
His unused bed looked strange to him. He got out of his
wrinkled clothes, put on his bathrobe, and called the hotel
again. This time Laura answered, and when he heard her
voice, his own faltered.

"Laura . . . how are you? I'm so sorry. . . ."

"Peter, you were a dear to go tramping around all night,
getting hold of those two. They've just called, one after the
other. You must be all in."

"I'm all right. Are the arrangements all made?"

"The arrangements . . . yes. Desmond has just been in
touch with them. Everything is done. I can't really chat
now, Peter. We have a lot of telephoning to do—cancelling
the trip . . ."

"Where is the funeral to be held?"

"It won't be a funeral, really. Desmond bought a plot

years ago. We had a little trouble, you know. The Long Island cemeteries are all, almost, Israeli territory. But he found one, for the nondenominational dead." She laughed, waited the space of a breath for his response, and when there was none, she said, "It's called Mount Laurel Rest, just beyond Queens, I think."

"This morning?"

"Not so fast," she said. "Even Desmond can't work that kind of miracle. It's at two. Desmond says the home is quite indignant with us. I suppose they think we're very low class. Officials are always vicious, aren't they?"

He wanted abruptly to end the conversation. "I'll let you make your calls then," he said.

"Peter, we can't thank you enough," she said very formally.

He called Clara. Since the funeral was supposed to be somewhere beyond Queens, it might be better if she met him downtown, here in the Village at the garage where he kept his car. He said about 12:30. Perhaps she could get a little more sleep. She didn't want to sleep, she said, her voice worried.

"Are you afraid?" he asked. "About being there with Laura in the cemetery?"

"Christ, yes!" she said, her voice exploding in his ear. "I hate it! I hate the way I feel about it! Well—I said I would go. So I will. But I don't know what I'll do if she throws a fit when she sees me."

"Bury her!" he said.

Her laugh was troubled, fearful.

"How did you manage it?" she asked. "Talking to her and knowing you'd been to see me, to tell me. . . . She always catches me out. I've never got away with it."

He didn't want to talk about how he'd felt, so he lied to Clara. "I didn't think about it," he said. "And she's not my mother."

He put down the phone and discovered his hands were trembling slightly. He and Clara had become co-conspirators. For Laura, he had always loosened what tenuous bonds held him to other people; his betrayal of them was his gift to her. Yet he rarely spoke of her to others—as though she was a secret, sacred object carried around his neck. She had been for him so singular, so unique, so unmediated, the very stuff of an essential humanness before it was refined and shaped by conciliation. About her, there had been no odor of sanctity, the sickly sweet smell of family life. Now he was conspiring to force it on her at the very brink of her mother's grave.

He had waked on Clara's couch with a backache, his head thick with the residue of anxious dreams. What he had said to Clara about Laura's lawlessness reverberated in his mind as he drank the coffee she prepared for him. What did those words mean? They had been elicited from him at a late hour, spoken in exasperation. They had not given any ultimate definition to his relationship with Laura. But they had exploded it. He knew how transient such dramatic summations could be, surging up with what seems to be all the truth of a thing, falling away as a great wave falls, into the trough of daily life and its unthinking motion.

As he bathed and changed his clothes, as he telephoned his office to say he would not be in that day, and ordered his car from the garage, he was thinking ceaselessly about himself. He could not bear the tremor in his fingers. He found his apartment cramped. It seemed to him that the

very simplicity of its furnishings was pretentious. If he
secretly accused Violet of claiming everything she owned
had fallen from the lap of God, untainted by human commerce, how could he not judge his own pretended simplicity? He remembered Eugenio's miserable, drab clothes
hanging from the metal rack. He stared with disgust at his
own navy blue suits. His secretary's lisping, overly sympa-
thetic voice on the phone implied years of unwarranted
and presumptuous leniency toward him. When she said
she hoped he'd feel better soon—he had, for some reason,
said he had a touch of flu—he thought for a moment with
a literally divided consciousness that she'd said she hoped
he would feel worse soon.

He drank large quantities of water, no sooner finishing
one glass than he felt dry again and went for another.

He would try to work. But when he took hold of a manuscript that was lying on his desk, it slipped from his hand
and fell to the floor, its pages scattering all over the rug.
He cursed it and himself, and glancing frantically about
the walls of his living room as though they were the walls
of a cell, his eyes fell upon Hansen's drawing of himself
and Barbara.

She had two grown children now. She was living with
her husband in Chicago. Sometimes he ran into people
they had both known and they gave him news of her. She
had married almost at once after their divorce. When he
tried to imagine her, she was always the young woman he
had married. But she was almost exactly his age, their
birthdays only a month apart. He had forgotten whose
came first. What *had* she been like? "Poor Barby," Laura
called her. Had she been poor Barby? Why had she married him? She had been so sure about wanting a divorce—

as he had been. And she had suffered. But she must have known that something hopeless was embedded like a stone at the heart of their marriage. Something about him.

He poured whiskey into a glass and sat down and sipped it slowly, and slowly he began to feel calm. He sat there for a while, then went and picked up the pages of the manuscript, and put them in order. It was still too early to leave for the garage, but he must get out of the apartment. He could stop by the neighborhood bookstore for a while. As he walked downstairs, he heard the sound of Violet's vacuum cleaner.

In the bookstore, several young clerks were gathered around a workman who was installing a mirror in a corner of a wall. The proprietor, an elderly man with a bramble of beard, his fat torso encased in wine-colored corduroy, said, "Well, Mr. Rice, you see what I have been pushed to do? They've been stealing me blind, coming in here and ripping off my stock. God knows the end of all this. There's more stealing than buying. Now, who's supposed to watch that mirror all the time?"

Peter looked up into the mirror. "See?" asked the proprietor, "you can see what's going on in there." Peter saw himself distorted, tiny, mostly head and gray hair, a glint of eyeglasses.

"I'll just browse," he said.

On the new fiction stand, he saw three novels from his own publishing house. One was by the Japanese writer. On the back was a large photograph of her wearing a kimono. She was looking directly into the camera, directly at him. He had paid scant attention to the picture when it was on his desk. Now he stared at it. All that was enigmatic about her had been wiped out by the camera. She was simply Oriental. When she came to see him the first time, she had been wearing a gray suit, a bag slung over her shoulder. It was ridiculous and wasteful of him to buy the novel, but he intended to, to give it to Clara.

The proprietor glanced down at it. "Things are bad all over, aren't they, Mr. Rice. You got to go out and buy your own books now?"

Peter said, "I wanted to see how it felt to be a customer. Don't put it in a bag."

He found Clara waiting for him on the sidewalk in front of the entrance to the garage. She was wearing a dark brown suit and a white raincoat.

"Is it a long way?" she asked.

"Not in distance, but maybe in traffic."

An attendant drove out the car and handed him his keys.

"Will it take long to get there?" she asked.

"It depends," he said. "You can't predict traffic anymore. Here's a book for you."

"Thank you," she said. "Isn't this the woman you were speaking about at dinner last night?" He nodded. "How foreign the Japanese are," she remarked. "More foreign than anyone. She's very pretty."

"The salesmen didn't think so. They didn't care for the book either."

"I've got two left-handed gloves," she said. "I grabbed them up without looking."

"It doesn't matter."

"I'd feel better if I was entirely covered," she said. "Are you supposed to wear a hat to a funeral?"

"I don't think anyone cares these days."

"God! I wish the rain would stop!"

They drove through the streets of lower Broadway, Clara talking of the lofts some of her friends had been digging out of the entrails of old warehouses or abandoned factories, he noting the variety and costly breed of dogs being walked by young couples on the narrow streets, where windows thick with dust and walls painted the dead green or gray of prisons seemed never to have been touched with sunlight. It was not so much a conversation as a sustaining of sound. Each was apprehensive, but Peter felt abashed too, humbled by daylight and weariness, the illumination, the purpose of the night now dwindled down.

Soon, they both grew silent. After they crossed the Williamsburg bridge, they made better time. There wasn't much traffic after all. As they neared an underpass, Clara said, "Look! Up there!"

On the bridge above, Peter glimpsed a number of bearded men walking, their large, black, flat-crowned hats all seeming to slant in the same direction.

"Hasidim," he said.

"How amazing they look!" she said. "Like creatures from a fairy tale."

"Do you know anything about them?" he asked.

"No. Just that they're a Jewish sect, aren't they? But it's like an omen, seeing them like that."

He glanced over at her. She looked absorbed, faintly gratified. He thought, she's still young enough to find a promise in diversity, to claim the promise for her own life.

"Did it go all right this morning?" he asked. "With your friend?"

She replied somewhat defensively. "He's very conventional. For a moment there, I wanted to tell him I'd go with him anyhow. He would have been shocked." She paused, then said, "It's odd to think that if I had gone with him, I wouldn't have told him about Alma's death. I would have kept it to myself . . . the way Laura did."

At the mention of her mother's name, Peter felt a thrust of fear.

"This will change things between you and Laura, won't it?" she asked, speaking quickly and without emphasis as though disposing of something that had little meaning for her but might if she thought about it.

"Yes," he replied bleakly.

"For me, too," she remarked. "Although I can't think how things can change between us. I don't know what there is to change."

By the time they reached the filigreed gates of Mount Laurel Rest Cemetery, the rain was falling in gusts. Above them, the sky seethed and rolled with thick gray clouds. The wind which had arisen blew their coats against them, blew across the fields of tombs around them, stirring the stiff clumps of plastic flowers that were set in front of some of the graves, their piercing reds and greens and blues like something acid on the tongue.

Peter left the car in a circular parking space from which graveled paths led to one section or another of the Mount, a barely perceptible rise in which young trees, their limbs black in the rain, seemed to have been stuck in the earth carelessly, like pitchforks.

A few hundred yards away, they saw two men talking, standing by a heap of freshly excavated soil. They began to walk toward them. Peter took off his glasses; they were too wet to see through. Clara buttoned her coat. Peter approached the two men. "Yeah," one said, in answer to Peter's question. He gestured toward the hole. "That's Maldonada. They're due along now."

Nearby stood a family sepulcher, its massive door open. One of the gravediggers gestured toward it. "You can go in there and get out of the rain," he said.

Clara looked reluctant. "Come on," Peter said. "We might as well."

They ducked beneath the low portal. The floor was earth. Shovels, pails, and a large wooden box were neatly placed against one wall. They sat down on a narrow stone ledge behind which rose three tiers of coffins. Shortly, the two gravediggers came to stand just inside the entrance. They muttered to each other, ignoring Peter and Clara.

"I've never been inside one of these things," she whispered.

"It's shelter," he said.

"I wasn't objecting. You could even say it's cozy."

Peter smiled. "You could," he agreed.

"I'm really scared," she said. He touched her hand.

One of the gravediggers turned to them. "Your party is here," he informed them, then he and the other man went outside and walked away to stand some distance from the open grave. Peter got up at once and walked out just as Carlos arrived at the entrance to the sepulcher.

"Peter! You came!" he exclaimed. Peter said nothing. Carlos peered inside to where Clara was still sitting, huddled, on the ledge. He stared at her for a long moment, then went on. In another minute, Desmond walked by, his arm around Laura, then Eugenio.

Clara went out. The branches of the trees were whipping back and forth in the wind. Some men, beetlelike in their black clothes, were carrying a coffin up the path toward her. She went to stand at the gravesite next to Peter. At that moment, Laura, with a look of revulsion, drew her foot off the carpet of false grass which had been thrown over the raw earth on the edge of the hole. Then she looked up and saw Clara and Peter standing together. Clara wanted to shriek.

But Laura said nothing, and her face was empty of all expression. She hardly seemed alive.

On either side of her stood Desmond and Carlos. A few feet away, Eugenio stared at the ground, his hands clasped in front of him, a plastic transparent cover on his hat. Carlos wore his beret. But Laura's head was bare and her hair, darkened by the wet, was plastered to her cheeks and forehead.

The coffin was placed in a metal cradle. The men from the funeral home stood back, their heads bowed.

There was no sound except the rain falling on gravel and earth. Everyone was waiting. Then Desmond whispered something to Carlos. "I don't know, really," Carlos said loudly.

Desmond stooped quickly and scooped up a handful of earth and threw it on the coffin. The funeral home men seemed to spring forward at once. The ropes that held the coffin were loosened and paid out, and the coffin dropped heavily downward.

Peter, half blind without his eyeglasses, looked across at Laura. Her eyes met his briefly; her glance passed over him. He might have been invisible.

In the box, nearly at the bottom of the grave now, was an old woman Peter had hardly known. Her three elderly children seemed to lean forward as though they too were drawn down toward what remained of their mother, a woman from a different time he would never know anything about. All around him, the gray pastures of the dead for an instant seemed to reverberate with the lost energies of unknown lives, and Peter felt the crushing weight, the sheer effort of a single human life to complete its course.

A few feet away from him stood Clara. She was staring at the ground. He could not imagine what she was thinking, why she had given in to him and come to this place, what she sensed, if she sensed anything, of the significance of her standing there with the others. And if her presence had no significance for her, then what did it matter that she was there? Had it really been for her that he had been so insistent?

The gravediggers were looking now with open calculation at the group around the grave. He looked once more at Laura. How shrunken she seemed! How miserably wet she looked! How like her not to have worn some covering for her head! He strained to see the young girl who had, so long ago, smiled at him in that disordered, lovely room on a spring morning.

Then, suddenly, she looked straight at him. Although her features were indistinct to him, he felt the force of Laura's whole self gathered up into that forward thrust of her head toward him, and he was shaken out of his perpetual effort to recollect her as he had first seen her.

"What you've done is nothing . . . nothing!" she said.

Desmond put his arm around her, gathering her up and pressing her against himself, and began to lead her down the path to the limousine that waited below in the parking space. Behind them, the two brothers followed. Peter turned to Clara. She was staring at him fixedly; he did not know whether she had heard Laura's actual words or not, but she must have caught the sound of that voice coming toward him like a squall moving swiftly across water.

The rain was slackening. He thought he smelled lilac. But it couldn't be lilac yet, not till late April. He watched Laura bend and get into the car, then Desmond, then Carlos. Eugenio sat in the front with the driver.

The gravediggers were walking toward the grave, their shovels ready. He stood another minute, aware of Clara's questioning glance.

"Wait!" he wanted to cry to Clara, to the gravediggers. "Wait! It's not nothing . . . I've almost got hold of it!"

But all that came to him was the fragment of a memory that like a dream faded even as he struggled to hold it—another spring morning when he was twelve years old, when he'd awakened in his bed by the window and seen, freshly fallen, the last thin snow of the year, heard, below in the kitchen, the voices of his mother and his sisters as they went about making breakfast, known the cat and dog had been let out because he saw their paw marks braiding the snow, and felt that that day, he only wanted to be good.

THE WIDOW'S
CHILDREN

Paula Fox

DISCUSSION QUESTIONS

1. At one point, Clara claims that: *"Families were not as they seemed. . . . Wasn't everyone damaged? she asked herself . . . and concluded that the house of Atreus was, and always had been, full of boarders like herself."* Do you agree with Clara? To what extent is the story of the Maldonadas a universal story?

2. The author uses names and naming as an additional literary device in the novel. Can you identify the names that are part of this word game? What does each add to your understanding of the novel?

3. In what ways is parenting an important theme in the book? For the Maldonadas, what is the main attribute of the parent-child relation? How does each character respond to this relation?

4. What role does money play in the story of the Maldonada family? How does each character respond to the notion of money?

5. In her introduction to the book, Andrea Barrett likens the Maldonada family to a Greek tragedy. What "tragic flaw" (or flaws) seem to shape the actions of this family? How does each character respond to it? Is there hope of change or redemption for the Maldonadas?

6. Both Clara and Peter appear to be different from the other characters, and to hold a different place in the novel's structure. Are Clara and Peter witnesses? Participants? A little of both?

7. What is Clara's role in the novel? Is she part of the Maldonada family, or fundamentally different from them?

8. What is Peter's role in the novel? Why do you think Paula Fox gives him such a prominent role toward the end of the book?

9. Who would you say is the hero or heroine in this novel? Does this novel have a hero or heroine?

10. What role does each character have in the novel, and how does that role change as the story progresses and we find out more about them? How do the characters, in their different roles and places in the novel, interact with each other to create an important statement about the differences between family identity and individual identity?

11. One of the main conflicts in the book is the conflict of emotion and restraint. Which characters represent which quality? How does Paula Fox illustrate the expression of emotion? According to your reading of *The Widow's Children,* is restraint a positive quality or a negative one?

12. In a highly favorable review of *The Widow's Children,* Peter S. Prescott wrote in *Newsweek* that while he greatly admired Paula Fox's work, he was not always certain he liked it. Can you think of examples from *The Widow's Children* which might explain this seeming paradox?

⇝ Praise for Paula Fox's *Desperate Characters* ⇜

"*Desperate Characters* deserves a second coming more than most books. . . . Fox's prose hurts. It's written on the nerves."

—Walter Kirn, *New York Magazine*

"A towering landmark of postwar realism. . . . A sustained work of prose so lucid and fine that it seems less written than carved."

—David Foster Wallace

"One of the few novels I've quite literally kept near me over the years, to reread regularly. . . . It's thrilling to see her book made available again."   —Rosellen Brown

"Using a merciless camera's-eye style, Paula Fox . . . spreads problems before the reader and makes no recommendation. . . . The skillful insistency with which Miss Fox probes her characters' lives holds one's attention."   —Peter Rowley, *New York Times Book Review*

"*Desperate Characters* takes its place in a major American tradition, the line of the short novel exemplified by *Billy Budd, The Great Gatsby, Miss Lonelyhearts,* and *Seize the Day.* . . . Grueling and brilliant."
                                    —Irving Howe, *The New Republic*

Available in Norton Paperback Fiction